ORACLE OF PHILADELPHIA

BOOK ONE: EARTHBOUND ANGELS

ELIZABETH CORRIGAN

Oracle of Philadelphia
A Red Adept Publishing Book

Red Adept Publishing, LLC
104 Bugenfield Court
Garner, NC 27529
http://RedAdeptPublishing.com/

ISBN-13: 978-1482692471
ISBN-10: 1482692473

First Print Edition: March 2013

Cover and Formatting: Streetlight Graphics

To Stephanie,
Without whom there would be no Jul

ANGEL HIERARCHY

Rank	Name	Virtue	Status
1	Lucifer (Satan, Sammael)	Glory	Demon
2	Michael	Order	Angel
3	Gabriel	Joy	Angel
4	Keziel	Balance	Angel
5	Uriel	Death	Angel
6	Sarakiel	Courage	Grigori
7	Lethe (Betzalel)	Mercy	Demon
8	Lilith (Lelial)	Vengeance	Demon
9	Mephistopheles (Baraquiel)	Intelligence	Demon
10	Siren (Zabethiel)	Honesty	Angel
11	Rachel	Justice	Angel
12	Nathaniel	Faith	Angel
13	Raziel	Hope	Angel
14	Beelzebub (Asmodel)	Generosity	Demon
15	Raphael	Innocence	Angel
16	Sybil (Tzaphquiel)	Patience	Angel
17	Somniel	Peace	Angel
18	The Beast (Gagheil)	Tenacity	Demon
19	Jophiel	Service	Angel
20	Azrael	Love	Demon
*	Bedlam (Azazel)	Chaos	Demon

CHAPTER 1

I FELT THE MOB TURN ON *me, and I tried to flee. I didn't make it more than a few feet before a pair of strong hands grabbed me and pulled me back. I wrested my arms away, but as I felt the first grasp weaken, another villager took hold and twisted me back to face the crowd.*

I struggled, but soon the townsfolk had me surrounded, the throng a dozen people thick in all directions, each soul eager to land at least one blow on my body. A dozen fists assaulted me, and as each hit, the thoughts of the assailant echoed through my mind.

Wretched girl.

Unholy abomination.

Murderer.

I wrapped my hands around my middle, anxious to protect the child growing in my womb. Even as I made the effort, I knew that the assembly would not cease their attack until long after my death, a release I was no longer sure the gods could grant me.

The first stone struck my temple, and a trickle of blood dripped down my face. I turned instinctively to see from what direction it came, but even as I did, I felt another rock hit me from behind. I fell to my knees, unable to stand under the bevy of fists and stones pummeling me. I looked up to see a large rock descending toward me. I closed my eyes and prayed it might grant me the peace of unconsciousness.

I sat up straight in bed, a scream dying on my lips as I realized I was in the small apartment I kept over my diner.

I took a deep breath and tried to slow my racing pulse. No matter how many centuries I put between myself and that rabid crowd, that dream still scared me like nothing else.

I ran my fingers through my sweat-soaked black hair and glanced at the clock on the table next to the bed. The glowing LED display and first hints of sunshine peeking through my windows informed me it was almost time for me to get up. I reached a shaking hand out to turn off the alarm and got out of bed.

I walked to the bathroom and leaned on the sink. I met the gaze of my large brown eyes in the mirror. The bags underneath them didn't look too bad. The light brown skin of my face seemed a little pale, but I was sure a hot shower would fix that right up.

And sure enough, by the time I put on my skirt and cardigan and blow-dried my curls, I looked like my old self.

The wooden steps creaked as I hurried down them into the main body of the diner. I flipped the switch and watched as the fluorescent lights flickered to life across the room. The diner wasn't much to look at, an L-shaped room lined with booths containing dented metal tables and teal vinyl benches.

I conducted most of the affairs of the restaurant from behind the silver counter, which was lined in front with four round teal stools. Or at least I did when I was fully staffed and not trying to act as manager and waitstaff.

I pushed open the swinging metal doors to the diner's kitchen. I sorted through the bread on the shelves and pulled out an English muffin and put it in the toaster. As I waited for it to heat up, the bell above the front door rang, and a few minutes later, my cook Dwayne stepped into the kitchen.

"Hi, Carrie." He pulled the white apron off the hook by the door and put it over his head. "Do you want me to make you something?"

"Nope. I'm good." I pointed toward the toaster, which obligingly popped out my breakfast.

She never lets me make her anything, he thought. I cringed at his disappointment. Dwayne was a nice guy, but I hired him more because of his desperation for employment than because of his exemplary skills as a cook. Despite my rejection, he seemed to be in good spirits. I could tell.

People had asked me any number of times what my power felt like, and I never quite knew how to describe it. Souls had an aura coming off them, but I could see the light even with my eyes closed. I felt emotions against my skin like a temperature, but the sensations were more than just hot or cold.

And I could hear other people's thoughts.

After I finished my breakfast, I went back into the diner and flipped the sign to "Open." As I walked back to the counter, the bell above the door chimed, and I turned to see Madame Zarita bustle in. The plump woman had strode into my diner a few years ago and claimed that my recently deceased psychic had spoken to her from beyond the grave and insisted that she come to my aid. After learning that Madame Zarita devoured the obituary section of the *Philadelphia Inquirer* with a voraciousness that most people reserved for Thanksgiving dinners, I suspected that my last spiritualist's recent write-up had more to do with Madame Zarita's arrival than any supernatural intervention.

But she was quite correct in thinking that I was in need of a decoy psychic. People were more comfortable with the concept of an all-knowing Oracle than they were with the actuality of one. I liked to keep my existence on a barely more than mythic level, and Madame Zarita, a kindly old lady who was almost sure to fail any skeptic's well-designed tests of her powers, constituted an excellent disguise.

I poured two cups of coffee and carried one back to Madame Zarita as she settled herself in her customary booth at the back of the diner. As I started back to the front of the diner, the bell over the door chimed as a group of students who looked as if I were their last stop after a long night came in and crowded into a booth.

Throughout the morning, I had what could generously be called a steady trickle of customers, which was how I could get away with waiting on all the tables myself. We'd had what passed for a lunch rush—two whole tables occupied at once—and I was clearing off the tables when I heard the words that were going to change my life:

"I'm here to see the Oracle."

I dropped the pile of plates I had cleared from a recently vacated table. Not because of the words themselves, though they were surprising enough, since only someone who had special knowledge of Heaven or Hell would know to call me by the moniker I hadn't used in centuries. And not because of the appearance of the man who had spoken. He was attractive enough, but not movie-star handsome. His nose was a little too big and his light brown hair a little too curly. Plus, I had always suspected that Hollywood denied auditions to any men who didn't have blue eyes, and the pair looking with dismay at the pile of broken porcelain and ketchup-soaked fries at my feet were decidedly brown. But he was ordinary-person good-looking, definitely above average for my clientele.

No, what stood out about him was his blinding goodness.

I had met many people in my eight thousand years, and most of them didn't fall neatly into categories of good or evil. Some people performed evil actions because of outside pressure or a desire to support their families. Others seemed good but quickly burned out or only bestowed their beneficence on the few they deemed worthy.

In the young man standing before me, there was no such contradiction; without prejudice or selfishness, he wanted only to make the world a better place for everyone. He might have had doubts over whether other people or his God would agree with his actions, but he would do what he believed was right in spite of that. Only once in

4

my long existence had I met a goodness that could rival the one that stood before me—in one of the most powerful of Heaven's angels.

"Oh my gosh! I'm so sorry!" the paragon of virtue said as he rushed forward to help me pick up the fragments of dishes. "I didn't mean to startle you."

I shook myself from the stupor into which his soul had shocked me. "No, it's all right. I've got it." I walked behind the counter to get my broom, but when I turned around, the young man had already picked up some of the larger fragments and was looking for somewhere to dump them. I pulled the small garbage can from behind the counter and brought it and my dustpan over to the mess.

I set the trash can near him. "Thanks for the help." I grabbed my grimy plaid dishcloth from where I had left it on the table so I could wipe the grease and ketchup off the brown linoleum.

He continued to pick up the bigger dish pieces and then held the dustpan as I swept the remaining mess into it. When we finished, I used the time it took to return my cleaning supplies behind the counter to gauge my helper's emotional state.

As I focused on the young man, I sensed an undercurrent of uneasiness about him. I had missed it in my first impression, either because I had attributed it to concern over the broken dishes or because I had been too blinded by his integrity. It only made sense, though; people rarely came to see me if they didn't have something serious weighing on their minds.

"What can I get for you?" I leaned my elbows on the counter, which I noticed was rather sticky and could do with a good wipe-down, probably with a cleaner rag than the one I'd been using on the floor.

"I'm Sebastian Connolly. I'm looking for the Oracle. I heard I might be able to find her here."

Most people wanted to see "the psychic" or said they

had a problem that required special help. I considered for a moment that Bedlam or Gabriel had sent Sebastian, but finally decided that was unlikely. The guy's decision to wear designer black slacks and expensive cologne to a diner that more commonly smelled of stale coffee and slightly rancid grease suggested that the hardest decision he'd had to make in the last year was whether to buy a Lexus or to spring for the BMW. People who came to the angels' notice usually had something more remarkable about them. Plus, in most cases, my friends were courteous enough to give me a heads-up before sending someone to my doorstep.

I glanced toward the back of the diner to see if Madame Zarita was still on the phone. She often told me that she thought cell phones were ruining America, but that didn't stop her from spending half the day cooing at her grandchildren and terrorizing her daughters-in-law.

Madame Zarita was working on a pair of yellow booties for the baby that her neighbor's daughter was expecting. Apparently, the daughter was both unemployed and unmarried, creating a huge scandal. Regardless, when I signaled to Madame Zarita that she had a client, she set her crochet down next to her on the aqua vinyl bench and gave Sebastian a welcoming smile.

Sebastian thanked me and turned away. I closed my eyes and took a deep breath, trying to absorb as much of the altruism radiating from him as possible. I liked to think I could store up good emotions and let them out when I was around an unsavory character. It hadn't worked so far, but that didn't stop me from trying.

The young man's hand trailed along the counter as he walked away, and I noticed a telltale mark that made me gasp. To the unknowing, the raised flesh could easily have been a scar from a childhood injury or the remnants of a burn. Someone with the right background, however, would notice that the careful swirl was too regular to have occurred by accident and could only mean one thing: Sebastian had sold his soul to a demon.

I had seen many such marks in my time, my own deal with Lucifer, which had led to my immortality being only the first. The devil and his six archdemons specialized in trading favors for souls, so at any given time, there were a hundred or so people walking the earth who had given up their chance of a heavenly reward in exchange for something more tangible on earth. Many of them became desperate enough to find their way to me.

The last person to walk into my diner in search of a way out of his demonic contract had been James Pierson, a baby-faced Vietnam veteran whose haggard expression hinted of atrocities that humans were never meant to see. He had witnessed the massacre of most of his unit and had sold his soul to Lethe in exchange for an early return home from the combat zone. When he visited me in the late summer of 1973, my heart had ached for his suffering, though I had to question the wisdom of trading an escape from one hell for spending an eternity in another. Yet I did what I had done for centuries: I turned him away. A few days later, I found a picture of James splashed across the front page of the paper. He stood next to a smiling woman and a little girl who had his eyes and her mother's curls. The corresponding article indicated that he had killed his wife and three-year-old daughter before shooting himself in the head. I tried to console myself with the thought that even if I had been able to negate his deal with Lethe, I couldn't have saved someone who had it in him to commit such a heinous act, but remembering the incident still brought tears to my eyes.

A hundred similar examples of lost souls paraded through my mind: William, who had wanted justice when the law failed to apprehend the man who raped and murdered his fiancée; Gladys, who sought to be the most talented singer in the world; Marcus, who strove to succeed his father on the elected council. People sold their souls for any number of reasons, some noble and some selfish, but every one of them had something in common: I didn't save them.

I used to try. I begged God to reverse the contracts, which He could have done without blinking, but I never received any evidence that He could even hear my pleas. Once or twice, I went so far as to attempt to persuade Lucifer to leave the people in peace, but he only laughed. Eventually, I gave up and accepted that I was powerless.

Just as I reached the conclusion that my wisest course of action would be to forget Sebastian's existence, I felt the arrival of a cluttered mind strong enough to overpower the thoughts from the doomed young man. I turned back to the counter. A black-clad man with black hair and black eyes had materialized on one of the stools. His grin suggested he had spent the last several hours wreaking havoc upon innocent passersby, and he wasn't quite done with his day yet.

"Hey, Khet," he said. "Have you missed me terribly?"

I rolled my eyes but was unable to help smiling back. "Yes, Bedlam. The last"—I glanced at the clock on the wall—"thirteen and a half hours that I have spent outside your company have been absolutely unbearable."

The demon's smile widened. "I knew they would be."

CHAPTER 2

FOR MANY YEARS AFTER BEING cast out of my village, I led a solitary existence. I eventually rejoined society, but I had a difficult time connecting with people on a meaningful level. I met the first person that I could truly call a friend while I served as an acolyte in a small temple to Isis in Egypt around 1200 B.C., performing minor roles and keeping tabs on the petitioners.

One day, I was performing a rite in front of the temple, looking out at the sands that stretched like a golden ocean as far as the eye could see. The noonday sun beat down on my head, which I kept bare more to fit in with my fellow acolytes than out of any devotion to a goddess I knew was a human reflection of some angel or other. A sense of great sadness permeated the small village surrounding the temple because the day before, a mother and son had died in childbirth.

Suddenly, I felt a presence that stood out from the steady hum of desolation coming from the village. The new mind belonged to some kind of angel, though I detected neither the sanctimoniousness of the angels nor the malicious cruelty of the demons. Instead, I felt a spiral of rotating emotions that left me dizzy enough that I had to put my hand against a stone pillar for a moment to steady myself.

I walked down the hallway, toward the new mind, past the grand images of the Mother of the Gods and the smaller glyphs that told the tales of her great deeds, and tried to sort through the cascade of images and emotions that filled my mind. Usually when I met someone, I could immediately sense a core to them, the thing most important to them, what they would die for; but in the new mind, all I received were a hundred conflicting thoughts struggling for precedence. The man's current emotional state similarly seemed to lack any center, though it cycled around guilt, confusion, anger, and a firm desire to be distracted from those three emotions.

"... terribly sorry, sir," a harried priest said to a figure slouched against a statue of Isis. The wings of the Queen of Heaven stretched out above the figure, as if she strove to protect him from anyone who would approach. "We have no oracle in this temple. That distinction lies with the temple to Amun over Siwa way. But please, let us pray to the goddess on your behalf."

The supplicant shook his head. That brief glance at his eyes was enough for me to identify him as a demon. He had black hair, golden skin, a slight build, and angular facial features. I found the combination striking. Angels got to pick their own forms, but neither angels nor demons had the power to change their black irises.

The demon scowled and shifted his weight away from the statue, much to the relief of the scandalized priest. "If I wanted to ask Keziel for something—and the degree to which I do not cannot be described in your limited mortal tongue—I would ask her." Underneath the bitter tone, I recognized the first stable piece of the maelstrom that was his mind. Keziel, whoever she was, meant something to him, more than possibly anything else in the world. His voice took on a slightly desperate tone as he said, "Wait a minute. You do talk to Keziel, don't you? Or more importantly, does she talk back? Has she mentioned me?"

The priest suddenly became concerned that the individual in front of him might have problems more serious than those that could be solved with prayer and looked around to see who was nearby to assist him, should the penitent become violent. "Sir, you seem to be deeply troubled—"

The demon held up his hand. "No, you're right. I don't want to talk about, think about, or have anything to do with Keziel." That was a lie, but one that he strove to believe. "No, I'm looking for the Oracle. Totally different person. Meph swore up and down that she was here, but sometimes he says this kind of thing to see what he can get me to believe. Apparently, I'm terribly gullible. Although other people vouch for her existence, as well..."

The demon evidently noticed that the priest looked at him as if he were a madman, and probably the kind that needed to be restrained by whatever means necessary. "You have absolutely no idea what I'm talking about, do you? Too bad, because I was hoping this would be my last stop. But I guess you can never trust an archdemon, can you? Thanks for your help." The demon flashed a smile, but his heart wasn't in it for more than a second or two.

As the demon walked away from the priest toward where I was hiding at the front of the temple, the priest debated whether or not he should stop the lunatic before he became a danger to himself or others, but erred on the side of hoping the man had simply had too much to drink.

I hid behind a column as the demon approached me. Should I make my presence known? I avoided the company of demons since, as a rule, they were evil and manipulative, two of my least favorite qualities. I tried to be sympathetic to them, but the simple truth was that they were wretched beings who liked to spread misery wherever they went. They had all rebelled against their Maker and then spent the intervening time in Hell, where generosity and selflessness were not exactly promoted.

I didn't get an evil feel from him, but that didn't mean I was eager to interact with him. As he approached, I experienced a sudden rush of disappointment bordering on despair.

I was so sure the Oracle would be here, he thought. *Is there even anywhere else I can look?*

Maybe everyone is right. Maybe she's a myth. And even if she is real, why would she help someone who has done the things I've done? I might as well crawl back into Hell and do whatever Belsy wants me to do...

"You know," I said before I even realized I intended to speak, "you're never going to get anything you want if you give up that easily." I stepped into the light.

He snapped his head to look at me. Even though he had sought me out, I expected him to dismiss me. People imagined the all-knowing Oracle to be older, taller, or in some other way more impressive than a bald young woman dressed in temple linens. On the few occasions I felt the need to identify myself and provide direct intervention to a soul in need, it often took me longer to convince the individual of my identity than it did to set him or her on the correct path.

However, the demon only needed to look at my somber expression for a moment before stating plainly, "You're the Oracle. I need your help."

I had no doubt he *thought* he needed my help, but I was unsure what assistance I could offer him. The most I could do for humans was point them in the right direction, and I had no idea what options were open to demons. But he knew what I was and still sought my assistance, so maybe he wasn't expecting a miracle. "All right." I motioned for him to follow me.

Some would argue that shutting myself into my bedchamber with a demon was a bad idea, but I wasn't concerned about being caught in an improper situation with a being who could make himself invisible to the average passerby, and my immortality made me unconcerned for my physical well-being. I thought it best that we talk somewhere private, lest someone discover who I was or—more likely—become angry with me for feeding the delusions of the mentally unstable.

The demon didn't bother to look around my sparse room. He threw himself down on my cot, almost knocking over the water carafe sitting on the table next to it. He propped himself up on his elbows and looked straight at me. "I'm Bedlam."

I kept eye contact with him as I pulled my wooden chair over by the bed and sat down in it. "I'm Khet." Whenever I moved to a new place, I gave myself a new name, something common to the region. I hadn't used my real name since I had heard it yelled by a hundred villagers throwing stones at me and beating me senseless.

Bedlam narrowed his eyes, thinking that if my name was really Khet, I couldn't possibly be as old as the Oracle he was looking for, but he didn't know anything about human naming conventions and figured it wouldn't hurt to tell his story one more time.

He sat up straight and faced me. "Okay, so here's my problem. You know how sometimes you start doing something, and it seems like a good idea at the time, but then suddenly there are dead bodies everywhere, and you're not quite sure how that happened?"

I couldn't see my face, but I was pretty sure my eyes were about to pop out of their sockets. *Maybe I was wrong in thinking he wasn't like the other demons.*

"Maybe I'd better back up."

"Maybe you'd better."

He looked away from me and focused his attention on a candle on the table next to my bed. He snapped his fingers, and a flame came to life on the wick. "I'm a demon. Specifically, the demon of chaos. Per the powers that be—a.k.a. Lucifer—I'm supposed to spend my time tempting people to do evil, so that's what I was doing. Trouble is, tempting people isn't that fun unless someone asks for something really interesting, like a few years ago when this one guy wished for a city made of gold. Where he even came up with the idea is beyond me; gold is not

13

very good construction material. But he wanted it, so I made the city for him. Unfortunately, there wasn't enough gold in his part of the world to make an entire city out of it, so I just put the city on the other side of the world and told him that someday his descendants would find it."

He frowned and stared harder at the candle. "Of course, people on that side of the world found it first and started living there, and they came to the same conclusion I did. Gold is pretty and shiny, but it's way too malleable for building. So the residents began slowly dismantling it. Meanwhile, the guy I made the city for has created this whole big ritual to pass the knowledge of the city down to his descendants, and they're all excited that they have this secret fortune, which I find a pretty good joke. I'll keep my word. They'll definitely find the city someday, but who knows if it will still be gold by then? I hope for the sake of continued evolution that they'll have realized that cities made of durable materials are better, anyway."

He reached out and started moving his fingers quickly through the flame. "Luci thought I spent way too much time in the golden city and decided to punish me by lending me to Lethe for a few decades. I must have made him really mad, because being forced to spend time with Lethe is pretty much the worst punishment I can imagine. Well, other than the Abyss, of course. Lethe and the banshees are so whiny. And they generally don't meet Lucifer's quota for evil done, so he sometimes sends others to do double-duty. But I don't even like to do single-duty unless it's for something really good, so instead of reporting to Lethe, I just decided to find something to entertain myself on earth."

"Entertain yourself?" I asked.

Bedlam nodded, his eyes bright. "Turns out there are a whole bunch of Hebrews who just got their freedom from Egypt, though I don't think they were particularly near here. Apparently, I missed a series of plagues, which disappointed me because there's nothing I like better than a good disaster. When I found them, the poor suckers were waiting for their great leader—Moses, I think they said his name was—to come back from communing with nature or the spirits or God or whatever. All I did was pretend to be one of them and mention to a few people that it might be nice to have a celebration to get spirits up again. And I might have suggested that they should make an image of God to thank him for releasing them from captivity. And I might or might not have put the idea into a few people's heads that God was a giant gold cow."

The words started pouring out of his mouth. "Now, let me say right here that it was all supposed to be a joke. I really didn't expect them to take it quite so literally. These were people who held on to their religion through generations of persecution and slavery. And a gold cow? Their religious texts say that God made them in His own image, so I thought they'd be pretty quick to dismiss that one."

"Not so much?" I asked.

He shook his head. "Nope, they bought the whole thing, and they actually threw a pretty good party, considering we were in the middle of the desert and resources were scarce. But then, Moses came down from the mountain and spoiled everything. Personally, I think he was just upset that we were having such a good time without him. Some people are so self-centered."

He scowled and looked away from me again. "Anyway, it all would have been fine if Moses hadn't decided that the best way to deal with his missing invitation was to go on a killing spree. He announced that everyone had a choice: refuse the cow god or face death. Well, that seemed like a no-brainer to me, except these people take their religion pretty seriously, even a weird cow religion they've only had for a few weeks. And you know, maybe they finally found the ultimate truth in the golden cow, or maybe they were just finally having some fun for once in their lives."

Bedlam flopped back down on the bed and stared at the ceiling. "So the people who weren't willing to give up the cow god were sentenced to painful and bloody deaths, whereas the 'true believers'—a.k.a. the ones who claimed that they absolutely had not been partying just a few minutes before—got to kill their friends and neighbors. It was the worst ending to a party ever."

I opened my mouth to say something soothing—like, "I'm sure it wasn't that bad"—but he continued before I could. "The ironic thing is, you know what Moses was allegedly doing during all this time? Getting rules passed down from God... or the voices in his head. I'm still not sure. Know what one of the rules was? *Don't kill people.* You'd think he'd have noticed the contradiction. Or maybe he did, and it didn't matter. Maybe it was only, 'Don't kill people who adhere to the exact same beliefs as you do. And by *adhere*, I mean claim to believe when the option is that or death.' Moses smashed the tablets before I got a chance to read the fine print."

He rolled up on his elbow and looked at me. "The thing is, I'm not really angry with Moses. He was just doing what he thought was right. He had brought these people to freedom in the name of his God, and they turned their back on that. It's no wonder he was angry." He lay back onto his back. "The one I'm angry with is me. This whole thing is totally my fault. I thought I was playing a joke, but it led to all those people being killed. And lots of dead bodies? Not so funny. You'd think I'd have thought of that before playing jokes on religious fanatics, but I just rushed right in without regard to the consequences. Like always."

"I'm sure that's not—"

"That makes me wonder what kind of consequences my other actions are going to have. Like what's going to happen to all the people in the city of gold when the descendants go looking for it? And I don't even want to think about what might happen with that really beautiful woman Azrael got me to make up in Sparta... Never mind."

He gave a heavy sigh. "Anyway, I've always pretty much thought I decided whether I was good or evil, regardless of what Luci and the others say. But I'm starting to worry that they may have been right all along. Maybe I don't really have a choice, and I'm just evil, after all."

He didn't turn to face me, and I wasn't sure if he was done or what I should say to him.

After about thirty seconds of silence, he pushed himself up on his elbow and faced me, his emotions spiraling downward. "That's a yes, isn't it?"

I frowned. I didn't recall him asking a question. "A yes to what?"

He turned his head away, and shame became the most prominent of his many emotions. "A yes that I'm evil."

"Oh." I wasn't in the habit of judging anyone as good or evil, much less angels and demons. I had been damned by the actions of others for as long as I could remember, and the only reason I wasn't burning in Hell was that, in the lingo of my current cohabitants, my *ka* was unable to separate from my body. And I had never been sure whether that was a hell of a different design. "I don't really think I can make that determination."

Bedlam looked puzzled, and his thoughts began to spin again, creating endless possible reasons for my answer. He rolled onto his side to stare at me. "You can tell things about me, right? You know someone better than they know themselves after looking at them once."

I nodded.

"Then why can't you tell me whether being a demon makes me evil?"

"I don't know that being a demon makes you evil. Demons and angels look pretty much the same to me, at least in your true form. Sometimes, I can tell from your minds because demons tend to be so full of hate and

17

desire to destroy. But I see that level of difference among humans too, and they're all still human. As far as I can tell, demons are angels who aren't allowed in Heaven, and while being kicked out of your home may have a profound effect on your psyche, it's unlikely to change your essence. I've been kicked out of many places that I call home, and I am pretty sure that I'm still human."

Again, I was struck by a smattering of his emotions: hope, self-satisfaction, concern that I was saying things to make him feel better. "So I'm not evil?"

I shrugged. "I can't say that either. I wouldn't necessarily describe tempting people to stray from their beliefs or creating golden cities for your own entertainment as actions of someone unassailably good. But really, I'm not the best person to judge that. I'm no more welcome in Heaven than you are."

Puzzlement, outrage, empathy. "I never heard that you were bound for Hell. The story goes that Lucifer collected other people's souls so that you might live, but that you weren't the one who asked for it."

Familiar frustration at the unfairness of my situation rose in my chest. "You heard the story correctly. But you must have missed the ending, where the Archangel Michael comes down and informs me that the evil actions of others on my behalf were sufficient to keep me from salvation, should the opportunity ever come my way."

He had even struck me with his flaming sword, leaving a burn mark on my arm that refused to heal, a mark that symbolized my expulsion from Heaven. I raised my sleeve to show Bedlam, but before I could, Bedlam's anger overpowered my senses.

He jumped to his feet and threw my water pitcher against the wall, where it shattered. "Michael! He wouldn't know who was or wasn't worthy of Heaven if he didn't have it directly whispered from the Lord! He didn't think *I* belonged in Heaven, and I'm sure he still has some special ceremony to celebrate I-Kicked-Bedlam-Out-of-Paradise day. I bet he serves those date candies I like, since I'm not there to have any!"

The intensity of Bedlam's fury made my mind feel as though it couldn't contain the strength of the emotions. The pressure built inside my skull, and my head began to throb. I worried that I might black out from the pain, so I closed my eyes and took some deep breaths.

Bedlam walked over and put his hand on my arm. "Khet?" His thoughts moved away from loathing and toward sympathy and fear for my health. "Khet? Are you okay?"

"I'm fine. Could you... tone down the anger a bit? Strong emotions can be a bit overpowering for me."

He hung his head and looked down at me with large black puppy-dog eyes. "I swear that I will never get angry around you again." *Yeah, because that's going to happen. Well, I can try.*

He teleported out shortly after that, and I had no idea what he was going to do with my advice, which had seemed more like random babblings than sage wisdom. He promised to come back to visit, though. I told him I wasn't sure how much longer I would be at the temple, but he said that he could track me using my unique chaos signature. Whatever that meant.

A few years later, I was living in a cave in Greece, acting as a hermit and wise woman, when Bedlam walked back into my life. He had determined that he was not returning to Hell and was going to do his very best to be good. At times, his very best left much to be desired, but all in all, there was always more good than evil in him.

Over the last three millennia, he and I spent increasingly large amounts of time in each other's company. I was usually content to stay in one place in Greece, Rome, Britain, or some other major civilization, but Bedlam always showed up, determined to break me out of my comfort zone and demand company for his latest expedition. He found passages through the unnavigable Himalayas so we could watch the building of the Great Wall of China. We braved the treacherous waters of the Sea of Japan to sample the flavors of Nippon long before people to the west added it to their trade routes. We heard lions roar across the grassy savannahs and rode the rapids through the jungles of the Amazon. He could have done any of those things on his own, of course, but he said that the world had more to offer when he had someone to experience it with.

Sometime in the Middle Ages, he decided to keep a normal human schedule and started sleeping at whatever abode I fashioned for myself, and he never quite gave up the habit. That was probably for the best, even though my tiny apartment overflowed with tiny knickknacks he purchased on his daily jaunts around the world. Neither of us liked to be alone.

CHAPTER 3

"**S**O HAS ANYTHING INTERESTING HAPPENED in my absence?" Bedlam asked. "And by that, I mean when did Gabs get back?"

I wrote down his usual order for pancakes, bacon, and coleslaw. I clipped the two-ply slip to the order wheel and spun it around for Dwayne. I reminded myself for the fiftieth time that I needed to put an ad in the paper about getting another cook to work on Dwayne's days off. I had put a sign in the window, but that hadn't gotten me any interest so far. Last week, Bedlam had tried to convince me I should post something online, but I didn't own a computer and wasn't sure how the Internet worked.

I picked up a rag and walked around the counter to finish wiping off the tables. "Gabriel's back?" I tried not to sound too excited at the prospect. Unlike Bedlam, my earthbound angel friend, Gabriel, did not spend the majority of his time with me. The average interval between his visits since I had bought the diner was about six months, but it had been well over a year since he had last stopped by. "Where did you see him?"

Bedlam didn't answer right away, and I turned to look at him. He pointed toward the other side of the room, and I heard the brass and wind tones of the Glenn Miller Orchestra's "In the Mood" fill the air. The antique jukebox in the corner hadn't played by conventional means for about twenty years, but that didn't stop it from belting out whatever tune Bedlam wanted.

He tapped his hands on the counter. "I saw an ad for swing dancing at Rittenhouse Square. We should totally go. We haven't been dancing in forever."

I turned back to the crumbs and bits of lettuce I was wiping off the table. "And when is this event being held?"

Bedlam stopped drumming, and I looked over my shoulder to see that he was counting out the days on his fingers. "Oh. I think it was last Saturday."

I shook my head as I moved onto the next table. "That may make it difficult for us to go, then." I was a little disappointed. It might have been fun to go out dancing. I felt as though I never left the diner anymore. Of course, when I tried to think of places to go, I came up blank.

When Dwayne placed Bedlam's order onto the pass bar, I picked up the food and served it. Bedlam didn't seem to notice that the pancakes were a little burnt as he spread coleslaw on top of them.

I pulled a mug out from under the counter and filled it from the regular coffeepot. "So are you going to tell me where you saw Gabriel?"

Bedlam took a moment to savor what he swore was the unequaled taste experience of pancakes and mayonnaise. When he spoke, his mouth was still full of what he had dubbed "the best BLT ever." "I didn't. You did."

He seemed content with that answer and began ripping open a jar's worth of sugar packets and upending them into his coffee.

"I didn't see Gabriel, Bedlam." If I were patient, he would eventually give me the information I wanted.

"Oh." His shoulders fell. "I guess I thought you did because you had that weird, calm look you get when he's around, like the sun is shining or you ate a really good empanada. Speaking of, did I tell you about my trip to Argentina last week? I wanted to see that cave with the painted handprints again..."

I let Bedlam babble on, though I wasn't so much listening

to his words or even his thoughts as I was allowing his constant stream of changing emotions to wash over me. Before I met him, I would have thought someone whose mind was so labyrinthine would give me a headache, but I actually found the undulating waves quite soothing.

"... and then the guy with the llamas claimed that he had been there first, and I said that was absurd because..."

Letting him do anything in the diner was another matter. One sweltering summer day a few years ago, my waitress called in sick, and my cook stopped showing up for work. I could have managed everything if my window air conditioner hadn't also broken, which made it so someone had to be a demon to stay in the kitchen with the fryer. In a rare moment of industriousness, Bedlam offered to do the cooking, and I could only assume that the heat had melted my brain because I agreed. The creative concoctions he prepared in place of what my customers ordered might not have been a problem for one day, but it took me a month to get someone to fix the air conditioner, and I couldn't in good conscience hire another cook to work in those conditions. By the time I got someone human back there, the clientele had gotten the word out that my diner served inedible food. I could have built my reputation back up, but I found it was easier to dispense oracular advice when I wasn't trying to manage a busy restaurant. Bedlam had told me I had the worst Yelp reviews in the city, whatever that meant.

"... at which point the gaucho pulled out a revolver, which you know always dampens the mood. I thought about letting him shoot me for the fun of it..."

Bedlam's arrival and the brief hope that Gabriel had returned were enough to distract me from the young man talking to Madame Zarita, at least for a few minutes. Bedlam's powerful angel mind blocked Sebastian's thoughts, an effect for which I was both relieved and disappointed.

"Khet? Are you even listening to me?" *Oh, light of*

23

Lucifer, I have become boring. My worst nightmare has come to pass.

I broke out of my reverie to find a hand being waved in front of my face. "Sorry." I focused my attention on him. "I'm listening now, really."

He sighed. "I tell you the fascinating tale of my adventures in the Pampas, and you don't even pay attention." He considered for a moment. "Which is fair, since I think llamas are overdone. You used to be able to mention a llama, and it would be the most random thing, but now everywhere you go, it's alpaca this, alpaca that."

"It's not that," I assured him.

"You're upset that I brought up Gabs, aren't you?" He looked at me with pathetic eyes that resembled those of a basset hound. "I'm sorry about that, but I really thought he must have been here, I swear, and... unholy Hellhounds of the Beast, that guy is one of Azrael's!"

As Bedlam was talking, Sebastian had walked across the diner and out the door, having apparently concluded his conversation with Madame Zarita. The demon twisted his body around to get a better look at the departing man, spilling his coffee all over his food and the counter in the process.

"I know." I hurried to wipe up the rivulets of coffee before they dribbled to the floor. "Well, I didn't know for sure that he was Azrael's, but it made the most sense. I take it from your response that you didn't send him."

"Khet, I am wounded." He didn't wait for me to finish cleaning the counter before he reached past me to grab the coffee pot. He dragged his arm through the area I hadn't cleaned yet and wound up with more of the brown liquid on his sleeve. "I know that I seem a bit unfocused and possibly not on the up-and-up as regards the whole moral divide thing, but I would never ever in a million—or at least three thousand—years send you someone who sold his or her soul. I learned my lesson after the first four or five times. Besides, even if I were to find someone dumb enough to sell his soul *and* smart enough to want your help *and* persuasive enough to get me to actually give away your location, I still wouldn't send you one of Azrael's. I do not mess with that bitch."

"Unlike all the other archdemons who you do like to 'mess with'?" I finished mopping up the coffee and threw the rag into a bin to wash later.

Bedlam wrinkled his nose. "Azrael is in a class of her own. She still thinks that because she didn't fight in the war, she didn't deserve to get cast out of Heaven." He reached down the counter to grab a fresh container of sugar packets. "I assume the boy came by to beg for a way out of his deal? Was it horribly pathetic? I know you hate listening to them—or rather, feeling whatever's in their heads—but I confess that I kind of get a kick out of their total inability to accept the consequences of their actions. I mean, we are talking about *eternity* in *Hell*. It's not difficult to grasp that this is something that no one wants, no matter what. I know, I know. You think humans can't understand eternity, but really, it isn't that hard. It's forever and ever and always, and you do *not* want to spend that in anguish."

"Bedlam, the fact that you're arguing for logic should tell you that you have no idea what you're talking about!" I didn't know what made me snap at him. After all, he was right, and I had been thinking the same thing. But I hated the callous way he put it, and I hated even more to have to associate that failure with the human who had just walked out my door.

Wow. I think she's only snapped at me, like, three times in the past. No, four, 'cause there was that time in Armadillo. But now that I think about it, that time had to do with demonic contracts, too. Maybe encouraging this train of thought is not my best choice here.

"I'm sorry," I said. "I just... think he must be at the

early stages, where he thinks there's an easy way out."

"Nope. His contract comes due any day now. I'd give him a month before Azrael comes for him." Bedlam spun around in a circle on his stool. "And if I may be so bold, if he's still in the city then, may I recommend that we not be? I've been dying to visit the Pacific. You know monsoon season is my very favorite time to travel. It's the only way I can get my chaotic violence kick without feeling bad about it."

"That can't be right."

"What? That it's monsoon season?" Bedlam stopped spinning and grinned at me. "I know you don't want to admit that Gabs has been gone for a whole year, but that really should not hinder our enjoyment of the inherent havoc of—"

I slammed my hand down on the counter, and Bedlam nearly fell backward off his stool. "Neither Gabriel nor your distasteful penchant for watching buildings get knocked over by tidal waves is going to distract me. What do you mean his contract is almost up? That's not possible, Bedlam. He couldn't possibly have spent even close to three years—"

"Okay, so you don't want to go to the Pacific. I guess I can respect that." Bedlam put his finger on his lips in a show of consideration. "I suppose I could be persuaded to go to the Alps. I need to practice my yodeling."

I sighed. Bedlam was right. But try as I might to forget Sebastian, he kept creeping back into my mind, and with him, thoughts of the first demonic contract I had seen fulfilled.

Eight thousand years, give or take, before Sebastian walked into my diner, I had walked home from the fair our village hosted with some of the neighboring towns with my husband, Hamin, and our friends Amie and Davi and their new baby, Vara.

"Don't you think that was the best village fair yet?" Amie was always cheerful, even after a day of carrying a fussy baby.

Davi laughed. "Yes, I love to watch Elder Rogan's face turn redder throughout the day as our village loses every competition."

"We won one this year. Hamin grew the largest onion of anyone." I gestured toward my husband, and he raised the prizewinning vegetable into the air.

Davi gave a whoop. "I'm sure the elders will be bragging for generations to come at our superiority in growing plants that make people cry."

Hamin nudged me. "Too bad they don't still have a village psychic contest. We'd have that one sewn up for sure."

I gasped and looked around to make sure no one had heard. "Be quiet. You know the elders don't like us talking about that."

Davi and Amie exchanged awkward glances. Everyone knew about my powers, but no one was supposed to talk about them. The village elders didn't approve of my ability to see into other people's heads.

Ami looked down at my belly. "You must be so tired. I know when I was expecting little Vara here, I would have been exhausted after walking around all day."

My cheeks warmed. My pregnancy had started to show a few weeks back, and everywhere I went, people still congratulated me. "My back does hurt a bit, but it will be worth it. At next year's village fair, I'll have a baby, and he and Vara can play together."

Amie lowered her voice. "Do you... Do you know that it's going to be a boy?"

I sighed. "No. I can't see the future. I'm guessing at this point."

"Hey, something's going on up there." Davi waved for the rest of us to hurry up.

As we crested the hill that led to the center of town,

two hundred or so villagers were crowded outside the public meetinghouse.

A powerful mind stood out to me. I stopped in my tracks. I had felt that mind before, when I was a little girl, almost too young to remember, but his visit had stayed with me. His return meant nothing good for our village.

My mother rushed over to me. "He's waiting for you! He asked for you by name!" She pulled at my arm and dragged me over to the crowd. The bodies parted, and I looked up to see the newcomer standing at the top of the semi-circular stone staircase that led up to the meetinghouse. He smiled when he saw me, but I saw in his mind that he loathed and feared me in equal measure, though I could recall nothing I had done to warrant the strength of his emotions.

I moved closer to the man, taking as much time as I could between steps, because I knew when I reached him, something terrible was going to befall me and everyone around me. The three village elders clustered to the angel's left at the bottom of the staircase, their expressions horrified.

He's really come, Elder Rogan thought. *Our sins have finally caught up with us.*

At last I reached the front of the crowd, and I took a position opposite the elders at the base of the steps. The man nodded. *The stage is now set.*

He gave a slight bow to the crowd, though there was nothing humble in his mind. "My name is Lucifer, and I have come to bestow a great honor on your village. My actions today will ensure that you will be remembered for all time. I have chosen to use the powers at my disposal to grant this girl eternal life."

A murmur came from the crowd, and they were uncertain what to think.

Who is this?

He must be someone terribly important.

What does he want with her?

28

Lucifer held up his hand. "I assure you, it is true. This is a deal I negotiated with your village elders some years ago, and now the time has come for all of you to pay the price. In exchange for my gift to your village, ten of you must come with me."

The villagers began to talk amongst themselves again, and Lucifer made no further move to stop them.

I didn't understand what was going on, but I felt that some action was required on my part. "No, thank you." My voice strengthened as I spoke. "I have no desire to be immortal."

Lucifer smiled, and even if I hadn't heard his malevolent thoughts, I could read the look in his eye. "Ah, but it is not up to you." He surveyed the crowd. "Now, let me see. Any ten souls I choose. Let us start with... you." On his last word, he made a gesture as if he were seizing something out of the air, and a shriek came from my right.

I turned; the crowd had moved away from a man lying on the ground. I recognized Eman, a man whose farm produced more food for the village than any other.

His wife let out a strangled scream. One of his sons knelt beside him and laid his ear on his father's chest. "He's dead."

The voices of the crowd grew louder in my head.
What? I didn't see!
Did he just kill that man?
That's not possible.

Eman's wife cried out again, and her daughter had to hold her to keep her from keeling over. Eman's standing son let out a roar and began to muscle his way forward.

I turned back to Lucifer. "Stop this."

The demon's grin widened. "Oh, I am just getting started." He made the grabbing motion again, but with both hands. The son kneeling next to Eman slumped over on top of his father, and the one pushing through the crowd fell like a dead tree into an unsuspecting woman, who backed away with a panicked look on her face and let out a series of choked gasps.

They're dead too.

We have to get out of here.

No, I want to see.

Some of the townsfolk began to back away, slowly at first, as if afraid to catch Lucifer's attention, but after they put a few feet between themselves and the crowd, they turned tail and ran. Still other townsfolk edged closer, their morbid curiosity outweighing their fear for their lives. I kept telling myself that it had to be some kind of dream, but try as I might, I could not wake myself.

"Now, see here." Elder Rogan stepped forward to address Lucifer. "You cannot—"

"I can do whatever I want." Lucifer's words carried none of the false pleasantries from a moment ago. "You made a deal. You wanted glory for your village, and it is time to pay your due." He turned back to the crowd and grasped the air again.

Who was it this time?

Oh, gods, was it me?

It doesn't look like anyone.

Everyone looked around, waiting to see who would fall next, and for a moment, nothing happened.

A scream arose from the back of the crowd. "My baby! She's not breathing. Someone help me! My baby!"

Amie! I looked around for my friend.

She shook her baby with increasing force, desperate to wake him. Davi moved forward through the thinning crowd and tried to rush Lucifer. The demon held up his hand, and it was as if Davi had run into some kind of transparent wall that he could not pass.

Lucifer laughed as Davi struggled against the invisible force holding him back. "By all means, keep fighting. I can keep this up all day."

A small boy, about two years old, toddled to the front of

the crowd and looked up at Lucifer with wide brown eyes. The demon knelt beside him. "Where are your parents, little one? They really should take better care of you."

"Errie! Errie!" The boy's mother pushed through the crowd, but too late. Lucifer waved his hand, and the child fell at his mother's feet.

I should do something, I thought. *Try to stop it like Davi or run with everyone else.* But I was frozen in place, unable to do nothing more than wrap my arms around my belly in a desperate effort to protect my unborn child. "Stop this! Stop this at once!"

Lucifer turned his eyes to me. "This is all done on your behalf. You should be more grateful, or I shall be motivated to punish you further." He reached out once more, and the next body to fall brushed the back of my legs as it landed.

Even before I turned to look, I knew I would see my mother on the ground. Time seemed to slow around me as I dropped to my knees and reached out trembling fingers to touch her frozen face. Her mouth was open, as if she wanted to tell me something, but whether it was a curse or a word of forgiveness, I would never know.

Someone called my name, and I turned to see Hamin pushing through the crowd. *No, go back*, I wanted to say. *Don't call attention to yourself.*

But he had already caught Lucifer's attention. He came within a few feet of me and collapsed. His prizewinning onion rolled from his lifeless hand.

I screamed inside my head, but I was too shocked to do anything more than stare at the vegetable that we had been laughing about only a short time before.

Lucifer counted on his fingers. "Let's see. The three farmers and the two babies make five, and the mother and the husband bring the total to seven, and that leaves..."— he turned to the cowering elders, and with three quick motions, finished them off, as well—"ten." He turned to look at me, a triumphant smile on his face.

31

"Why?" My hoarse voice sounded far away to my ears. "What possible purpose could this misery serve?"

He said nothing, and I didn't expect to be able to pull anything from his mind other than the smug satisfaction he appeared to get from the suffering of others. But a question was prominent in his mind: *Is it still true?*

And then I remembered what I had said to him ten years ago. "That's what this is about? All this because of the words of a child?" I stood and looked him in the eye. "Well, you didn't get what you wanted, because it is still true. It will always be true, no matter what actions you take."

He scowled. "Enjoy your immortality."

He disappeared.

Lucifer's angel mind had dimmed the emotions of the crowd, and when he left, the ire and grief and fear and powerlessness of the townsfolk flooded over me.

He's gone. Thank the gods.

How could this have happened? He said the leaders did something.

He said they did it as a favor to her. *This is all* her *fault.*

I realized then that as bad as things were, the situation was about to get much worse.

"How about Madrid?" Three days after Sebastian had visited my diner, Bedlam was still trying to convince me that we should take a vacation. "You love the chandeliers at the Palacio Real!"

I looked up from the pile of brown-specked dishes I was drying with the ShamWow he had picked up for me. I didn't own a television, and he had never grasped the mechanics of the post office, so I had no idea where he'd gotten it. Sometimes, I found it better not to ask. "Bedlam, if we're going to go on a trip, which I have conceded is not a bad idea, don't you want to go somewhere we haven't already been?"

He nodded, then bobbed his head to the '50s pop playing on the jukebox. "Barcelona! You've always meant to see the Sagrada Familia!"

My hands slowed as I wiped the inside of a coffee mug. "The plan was to go when it was done, but I suppose that will be close enough to never that we needn't delay the trip any longer."

Bedlam grinned and took a bite of his strange concoction of marshmallows and tomatoes. "And while we're there, we might as well hop across the Mediterranean and see Rome."

I put down the mug I had been cleaning and picked up another. "I don't know. I don't want to be away for that long. Someone might need me." *Like Sebastian.*

"Aw, come on. We could do a whole Mediterranean cruise. You've always wanted to do a cruise, and I'm sure they're full of lots of people who need your help." He bounced on his stool and clapped his hands. "We can finish in Greece and go see if your cave is still there!"

"I'm sure that whole area has been built over by now." But I had to admit the idea of a long vacation was appealing. "Maybe—"

A presence appeared next to Bedlam that made me feel as though the sun were shining on my face after a long, cold winter. Bedlam scowled and grumbled that we wouldn't get to go on vacation after all, but I couldn't bring myself to care as I turned toward the source of radiant light.

"Hello, Cassia," Gabriel said. "Did you get the referral I sent?"

CHAPTER 4

WHEN I MET GABRIEL, I was working at a tavern in Rome in the early years of A.D., though we didn't know that at the time. That particular morning, I had the simple task of serving travelers who were waylaid there, but as the sun reached its peak, a number of the locals arrived to enjoy spiced wine and the company of their neighbors prior to the gladiatorial bouts scheduled for that evening.

I disliked crowds on the best of days, and not just because of the raised temperature caused by the sweaty bodies or the yelling of drunken men trying to outdo one another's tales of bravery. I could feel the force of every soul clamoring to get my attention, striking me from all directions in an assault of thought and temperament. I had to concentrate to tell which emotions belonged to the foul-smelling gentleman placing his hand a little too close to my breast.

Arena days were the worst. The throng was desperate for a taste of violence, but the men were forced to whet their appetites with drinking and dice until the amphitheater opened. The usual barrage of human emotion that flowed into me was painted red by the vicious desires of those thirsty to witness violence stronger than the cockfighting that went on in the tavern garden, most nights. The bloodthirsty thoughts wormed their way through my brain and left me with both a throbbing headache and a short temper.

I shouldn't be working today, I thought as I delivered drinks and grapes to a table of men who complained that the tavern was far inferior to the one they usually frequented. One stated that the better place served liver and onions in addition to our more basic fare.

I picked up an empty plate from another table, and a man coughed on my hand, leaving flecks of spittle. I tried not to make a face as I wiped my hand on my tunic. I was fortunate to be immune to human disease, but that was half the reason I had come to work that day. My employer, Gnaeus, usually allowed me to stay home on arena days, but since half the staff had contracted the fever, he had begged me to come in and work. I had conceded because I hadn't served on an arena day in so long that I'd forgotten how strong an effect the crowds had on me.

Something boiling hot dripped on my foot. I jumped and shouted in astonishment, nearly knocking over a few patrons. The new tavern girl had dropped a cup of hot water, and it had shattered on the floor, splashing me and everyone in the vicinity.

"Watch it, Julia!" I yelled. "And clean that up!"

"I'm so sorry, Cassia!" Her innocent shame washed over me as she knelt on the dusty floor to pick up the fragments, her emotion a palpable contrast to the other feelings in the tavern. Poor girl. She was only doing the best she could with the little experience she had, and I bit her head off. I needed to get out of there.

As I was making my way across the crowded tavern to tell Gnaeus that my departure was both necessary and imminent, I felt the force of an icy angelic personality overwhelm many of the minds in the room. Ordinarily, I would welcome the presence of any angel or demon in such a moment. I would far prefer to hear the distasteful machinations of an inhuman mind than ordinary humans craving a brutality far worse than any that could be imagined by a demon.

Unfortunately, one kind of powerful mind could make such a scenario worse, and that was the overpowering disdain of someone who thought that I was far baser than the vicious souls from whom I wished to separate myself.

Sure enough, I looked toward the front of the tavern and saw the Archangel Michael standing next to the bar, looking far more attractive than someone so unpleasant had any right to, with his broad shoulders and thick dark brown hair. He glanced around the room. I could hear his thoughts as if he shouted them in a voice that could drown out the bustle of a public house full of intoxicated men. *Where is she? Somewhere in this cesspool, Toriel claimed. I need to find her and get her—and myself—out of here.*

I didn't know why Michael was looking for me, but I realized that I had two choices: push my way through the crowd to exit the building and force an immediate confrontation with Michael, or hide in the back of the tavern and hope he would leave soon. In retrospect, I should have chosen the former. Michael was a judgmental bastard, but his goal was the same as mine—getting me away from the building. Besides, his ability to maintain his current position in the crowd would almost certainly outlast mine, since his mind wasn't being assailed from all directions. But at the time, I lacked the clarity to distinguish among probabilities and elected to try to wait him out.

I slipped into a corner at the back of the tavern, where I was hidden by the open door leading to the roofed garden. I cowered there for about fifteen minutes. During that time, the crowd grew and became more raucous, increasing the distraction contributing to my indecision. Eventually, the tavern got so busy that Gnaeus was forced to abandon his post to locate his wayward employee. I didn't even notice him until he stood in front of me, gently shaking my shoulder and calling "Cassia!" for what seemed not to be the first time.

"I'm sorry," I said, looking at him and trying to focus.

"I'm sorry; I should be working. Just give me a minute..."

"Cassia, are you all right?" *Oh, no,* he thought. *She can't be sick now. I need her.*

Heat rose to my cheeks. I had put my desire to avoid Michael ahead of my employer's need to serve his patrons. I pushed myself away from the wall I hadn't even realized I was leaning against and wobbled a bit before my vision steadied. "I'm all right." I tried to give a reassuring smile, but I feared it resembled a grimace.

"Are you sure that you are not ill, Cassia?"

"No, no, I'm fine." I stood up straighter and made what I hoped was a better attempt at a smile.

I don't know. She looks better. And if I leave Julia out there alone, she's going to drive off half my customers. His own desperation decided him. "Why don't you go wait on those people over by the front entrance? I don't think Julia has gotten to them yet."

I held my shoulders back as I strode across the floor until I was within speaking distance of the group. At that point, I looked up to meet Michael's ice blue eyes. His cold mind became even stronger, and for a brief span of time, the crowd was almost silenced. I saw the hazy white glow of an angel in spirit form appear over his shoulder, and he turned his focus from me to the new arrival. I stumbled as the thoughts and feelings of the humans again rose to the forefront of my mind.

I expected to fall to the dusty floor, or perhaps crack my head against a wooden chair or table, but arms appeared from nowhere and caught me. At the same time, I felt the most amazing things, like a burst of sunlight shining into the tavern: love, joy, and goodness in such purity and abundance that everything else was muted.

I clutched the arm of the man who was attempting to help me keep my feet and had time to gasp, "Don't leave me," before I fainted.

"... am telling you this is a bad idea, Gabriel."

I awoke to the feel of a woolen blanket wrapped around me and a presence shining like the summer sun on my face. I was encircled by feelings of love and peace in a way that I had not been since my mother tucked me into bed as a small child, all those thousands of years ago. I thought to slip back into sleep, but the harsh, clipped voice and the wintry presence that provided a steady undercurrent to the light one dragged me into consciousness.

"Should I have left her there?" another male voice asked, a melodic baritone that blended with the sunlight suffusing the room. "She was ill, like many of the people in this town. Even if I didn't care about her, I couldn't leave her to infect others."

I assumed the second voice belonged to Gabriel, whoever he was. I rolled the name around in my head, trying to remember where I had heard it.

He's right, the cold mind thought. *She does not deserve your notice, but the other people there did.* "The disease is a mild one; people aren't dying in large numbers. Besides, she doesn't have the disease; she can't get sick. Whatever her problem was, I'm sure the other people there could have handled it." *Great, now he's giving me that disappointed look. Why do I always feel like I'm not living up to some standard with him?* "Okay, fine, but as you have now saved her from her possibly-nefarious fate, there is no more reason to remain here."

I felt as though a few scattered clouds drifted in front of the sun, blocking its rays.

Gabriel replied, "I need to talk to her." *She's the only thing left in this world to give me hope.*

For a moment, I almost believed that if I could stay in the presence of that light soul, so full of everything that I ever longed to feel, I could help it grow past the sadness into something even more beautiful, something that would make the world fall to its knees and marvel at its perfection.

But when the hostile speaker responded, I was jerked back into reality. "And I am telling you that you do not. Her very existence is founded on what we have been fighting for millennia." I recognized that voice. Only one man found me so unbearably dreadful that his regard made me feel as if I had been out in the snow too long.

"Michael, please." Gabriel's light lowered even further under the weight of the other angel's disapproval. "It's been so long since someone has been able to see inside of me. I need to know whether I'm on the right course, whether I'm even who I think I am anymore."

"You're being absurd." Michael's certainty radiated from him in a cold wave, even as Gabriel's warmth faded. "You are exactly who you have always been. Angels don't change, and we certainly don't question God."

Gabriel's amusement raised the psychic temperature of the room a bit. "The very fact that we are having this conversation yet again is sufficient evidence that you continue to believe it. And perhaps you are right. Perhaps I have no choice but to continue my existence as I always have. But it's been so long since someone has been able to tell me anything about myself. Lucifer is the only one with that power, and he's no longer available for consultation."

"Exactly. The power to see inside of others is now associated with the adversary. We all appreciated it when we had it available, but those days are gone." Michael's voice rose with increased vehemence. "Her continued existence comes only from Lucifer's machinations, and since she is in possession of a gift that previously only he possessed, he must have bequeathed it upon her in order to bring evil into this world..."

I had argued more than once with Michael over his insistence that I was a creation of Lucifer's. I had no evidence one way or the other. No one knew the limits of Lucifer's power, only that it exceeded that of every other angel. I had been forced to admit a long time ago that Michael could be right and that I had been forsworn by Heaven. But I was also well aware that it didn't matter whether I was slated for Heaven or Hell. Long after the last battle, I would still be forced to walk the earth alone. Michael, however, saw my attitude as further proof of my intrinsic corruption, since in his mind, any decent human sought Heaven above all else.

"... and those of us still on the side of light have spent all of our time trying to squelch the iniquity in which mankind repeatedly engages. Long ago the blood of an entire village stained her soul, and she has done nothing to wash it out..."

I rather wondered at Michael's ability to make those tiresome speeches. As the second most powerful angel in all of creation—one of the three archangels, along with Gabriel and Lucifer—he could order everyone to listen to his orations, and they would be forced to obey. But I would have thought that after so many millennia of listening to the same things over and over, someone would have had the courtesy to inform him that he sounded pompous and overbearing, not to mention increasingly tedious. Maybe angels, who unlike me had been *designed* to live eternally, were less interested in economy of language. Regardless, I had only seen one individual besides myself interrupt Michael when he got on his high horse.

"... behaves with disrespect toward the highest-ranking members of the host, willfully consorts with demons..."

I'd had enough of listening to the catalogue of my failures in the eyes of Heaven's chief enforcer. "I consort with *a* demon. One. Singular. And he at least has the decency not to malign my character in my presence."

The astonished silence that followed was more pronounced than my response warranted. Then I remembered that, as far as the arguing archangels knew, I had been unconscious. Sometimes I got so caught up in other people's discussions and emotions that I forgot I was not actively participating in the conversation, at least not from their perspectives. I sat up and tried to scowl at Michael, who was leaning against the wall by the arm of the sofa I lay on, but Gabriel was providing the room with such a soothing ambience that I found it difficult to hold the expression.

I regretted my words when I realized my chastisement had caused Gabriel's light to lessen a little bit more. I turned to capture my first glimpse of the archangel. All angels are good-looking, of course. And maybe I was influenced by the fact that I found his soul incomparably beautiful, but it seemed to me that there was a special attractiveness to his features as well. The Greeks and Romans of the recent ages had fashioned their gods primarily upon the behavior of the demonic, but I was sure they had chosen the appearance of their most stunning deities from the visage of Gabriel. Pale golden curls fell around the curves of his face, which managed to be both gentle and strong, and his cornflower blue eyes displayed none of the coldness I had come to expect from his fellows. He stood in front of a window facing west, and the setting sun provided backlight at the right angle to make him appear to have a halo like angels of legends.

"I apologize for our behavior." As Gabriel spoke, I realized his facial expressions, words, and thoughts were in complete accord with each other. Most people tempered their words into something more socially acceptable than their thoughts, but Gabriel seemed to have no such need. "It was unconscionable for us to speak so. My name is Gabriel, and I believe you know Michael."

"I'm Cassia. And I didn't mean to imply any offense. I'm grateful to you for getting me away from the mob."

The corners of Gabriel's mouth turned upward. "It was

nothing, really. You were clearly suffering. I'm sure anyone would have done the same."

"I'm sure you're right."

She's trying to charm him, wicked temptress that she is. Michael's hostility was so intense that I could have felt his glare boring into my head even if I didn't have oracular vision. *She knows as well as I that most people can't be bothered to help anyone but themselves. And that's to speak nothing of wasting the intervention of an angel on one suffering girl, especially one such as her.*

Michael was right, much as I hated to admit it—about humanity, not about me being a wicked temptress. Most people couldn't stop focusing on their own woes long enough to see someone else's distress, much less bother to help. But at that moment, I really wanted to believe what Gabriel believed, that people were unfailingly good and helpful. Besides, even if my firsthand experience inside others' heads prevented me from embracing his optimistic view of mankind, I couldn't bear to be the person who did anything to scar the archangel's bright and buoyant spirit. "You wanted to talk to me?"

"No," Michael's tone brooked no opposition. "In fact, we have already spent more than enough time here. We have extremely important matters afoot, and Gabriel and I both have responsibilities."

"I'm staying here, Michael." Gabriel's voice displayed none of the steely resolve of Michael's, but I knew he was not going to be persuaded to back down from his decision. "I need to talk to her. I'll—"

"Michael!"

I didn't recognize the newcomer, whose mind struck me as resembling a firework with bits of energy shooting off in all directions. His physical form was younger than that of other angels I had met; he appeared to be in his late teens. But like every other angel, he was beautiful, with curly red-gold hair and large blue eyes. He must have

42

been millennia older than I was, but he had an innocent childlike air about him that made me feel every one of my six thousand jaded years.

At the moment, however, the angel was red-faced with hysteria. "You have to help me! You have to make him stop! I can't do what I'm supposed to if he keeps interrupting!"

"Raphael, what are you doing here?" Michael asked. *And how many more things are going to go wrong today? We are in the middle of the most important event in history! This is no time for Gabriel to neglect his duties, and it's definitely no time for Raphael to prove his incompetence.*

"I tried to do what you said!" Tears formed at the corners of Raphael's eyes. "I delivered the Good News to some people so they would know that salvation is at hand. But he kept interfering, and I couldn't make him stop, and I don't know what to do."

A laughing presence materialized next to me. "Khet, Khet, Khet, Khet, Khet!"

"Bedlam!" I wrapped my arms around my friend. I leaned my head on his shoulder and felt the light wool of his toga rub against my cheek. "I missed you."

Touch always increases my sense of a person, and I had long sought refuge from the world by engulfing myself in the maelstrom of Bedlam's thoughts. The familiar cacophony calmed me. Gabriel's emotions were pleasurable, but there was something even more satisfying about being near my oldest friend and immersing myself in his thoughts. *I should have figured out a way to get some camels into the scene. Nothing says "birth of our Lord" like camels.*

"Bedlam!" Michael echoed my cry as he concluded that Bedlam was the "he" that had driven Raphael to tears. "I should have known that you would be interfering in the Lord's work. Get thee behind me, fiend!"

"Points for the melodrama, Michael, but I must point out that you are wrong on two counts," Bedlam said. "Well, I'm sure you are wrong on scads of things. But I am going to do you a favor and only discuss the two that are relevant at the moment. First, I am not a fiend anymore; Belsy officially kicked me out of his society a few centuries back. Since no one else would take me, I now identify as an unclassified demon. Or you know, fallen angel, which is the term I have always preferred. Second... I've forgotten second. What was second?" He looked to me for an answer.

"You were helping," I replied, reminding him of what had been in his thoughts. Then I realized what I had just said. "Wait. You were helping?"

"No!" Raphael wailed. "He was ruining everything! I was just trying to bring tidings of joy to some shepherds—"

"And that was your first mistake," Bedlam said. "I mean, seriously, shepherds? You have literally the biggest news of all time, that the Son of God is finally coming to earth to redeem humanity from their sins. You might or might not recall the giant war we fought over the issue a few thousand years back. One would think that you would want a lot of people to know about this. So what do you do? Go to the most populous location you can think of? Inform the people most likely to spread the word? No. You go visit three people who spend most of their lives alone with sheep and tell them. That's not even going to get a decent rumor started."

"I was looking for people pure of heart!" Raphael wrung his hands. "But I don't know who's pure of heart. No one but Lucifer can see into people's hearts. I told you I didn't know what I was doing."

Bedlam shook his head. "And let's pretend for a minute that these shepherds are the best people to relay this information to. You have to present it better. I mean, I can see going with the overly preachy language to emphasize the import, but why send only one little angel? You have to get a whole chorus going."

I nodded. That made sense to me, but then, I could feel the sincerity radiating off Bedlam. Michael's face, on the other hand, was growing redder by the minute.

44

Gabriel's eyes looked as though they might pop out of his head. "What did you do, Bedlam?"

Bedlam shrugged. "I just added a few angels flying in the sky. And they sang happy things. *Gloria in excelsis Deo* and such. Totally in keeping with the theme."

"But angels *don't have wings!*" Raphael's voice raised in pitch at every word until he was close to shrieking.

"People don't know that, Raph." Bedlam patted the frazzled angel on the shoulder. "I was just trying to encourage the whole image where angels and Heaven are up in the sky. It's way more appealing than going into the ground when you die. Trust me on this one. Anyway, I then realized that it was totally pointless of you to make this announcement without giving people directions, so I put a star over the stable and told them to head that way if they wanted to see him."

"You did what?" The icy force of Michael's wrath stung my face and drowned out everything else. "I should have expected something like this of you. Even Lucifer had the decency to agree to neutrality for thirty years after the birth. But you had to prove that you don't listen to anyone... yet again."

I clung tighter to Bedlam, trying to shut out the anger.

Huh. I didn't think it was that big a deal. Maybe I shouldn't have done it... but I'll never admit that to him. "Dear gods, Michael. Don't you think you're overreacting a bit?"

"Gods?" Michael asked, ever oblivious to attempts at baiting him. "Have you fallen so low that you do not even acknowledge the One True God anymore?"

"When in Rome." Bedlam's self-satisfied smirk would have made anyone want to slap it off his face, and he aimed it at Michael.

"You miserable demon." Michael advanced on Bedlam, causing both of us to lean back. "The Archdemons may have set themselves up as demigods in this heathen society, but to liken them to He whom I serve is unconscionable. Would that I could cast you someplace even lower than the pit for the constant blasphemy of your mere existence!"

"They worship you too, you know," Bedlam said. "They just think you have a lightning bolt instead of a flaming sword. And that you're a serial rapist. Any comments on that?"

From the look on Michael's face, I could have sworn he was actually going to hit Bedlam.

The smile fell from the demon's face, and he opened his black eyes wide. He held up both hands. "Mercy."

He looked perfectly sincere, but he was only goading Michael further. I tried warning, "Bedlam..."

A wave of cold fury emanated from Michael, dropping the temperature in the room. I shivered and pulled away from Bedlam to wrap my arms around my chest.

Michael glared at the demon, his blue eyes like sharp icicles. "Much as I would love to continue to discuss your ever-increasing desecration of all that is decent, I apparently have some miracles to manage. Come along, Raphael. Gabriel, I trust that you've seen the error of your ways and will also be reporting to me shortly." With a final glance at each of his colleagues, Michael disappeared.

Raphael looked confused for a moment and then followed.

Bedlam shook his head. "What was that all about?"

I tried to give him a stern look. "You didn't have to provoke him, you know. He might not hate you so much if you didn't repeatedly antagonize him."

Bedlam laughed, but there wasn't any joy in it. "Don't kid yourself. Michael and I have never been able to stand one another, and I don't see that changing in the near future. Or distant future. Or any future, except maybe one where everything was the opposite of the way it is now. But then, Michael would be a demon, which would almost certainly make his head explode. So it would really just be me not hating his memory, not us not hating each other."

He cocked his head to the side. *Hmm. But if everything were the opposite of the way it is, the sky would be the ground, and we couldn't walk on it. And snow would be hot and would have to melt itself, unless boiling was freezing, but at some point, wouldn't that make everything exactly the same as it is now, instead of opposite?*

I poked his arm. "Did you have a point in there somewhere?"

"Maybe?" He thought for a second. "Oh, right, I was wondering why he was so upset about the star thing."

"Because now the unrighteous know where God's Son is," Gabriel said. "Think about it. We want the world to know that the Son of God is coming to earth to save mankind from its sins. We want the faithful to be able to prepare. However, we are not so naïve as to think that everyone will accept the news graciously. People who don't understand will see Him as a threat to their power or a means to gain things for themselves. He's just a baby right now. He can't defend Himself or understand what He is. Until He's older, He needs to appear to be a normal baby with a normal family. You just broadcasted His location to the known world."

"Oh. I don't know why Michael didn't just say that. I'll be right back." Bedlam disappeared and then reappeared almost immediately. "There, it's gone now. No permanent damage done. Probably."

He grinned at me and was about to say something, but he got distracted by recognizing— "Gabriel!" He ran over and hugged the very surprised angel. "I haven't seen you in forever! How have you been? What are you doing here?"

Gabriel raised his eyebrows as he pulled away. "I might ask you the same question."

"Which question? How have I been, or what am I doing here?" Bedlam laughed, ignoring Gabriel's reluctance to interact with him.

Bedlam had told me long ago that he had never been

especially popular among his fellow angels, even before he decided to assist Lucifer in his rebellion, so he generally didn't let it bother him. By his standards, Gabriel's cautious aloofness was akin to offering up his firstborn.

Bedlam continued, "I came to tell my good friend Khet here about my assistance in Heaven's ultimate plan. And, you know, to mock Raphael's pathetic attempts at mass communication. I definitely wasn't expecting you or Michael to be here."

"Well, I don't think he was expecting to be here either," Gabriel said. "He knew that I was trying to find the Oracle, and I think he wanted to head me off."

"Seriously?" Bedlam looked over at me, bemused. "Michael hates you so much that he takes a break from his all-important plans just to stop someone from talking to you?"

"Yes, well..."

Bedlam shook his head and turned to face Gabriel. "So what are you doing here, Gabs? Interested in joining the proud few who stand against the almighty leader of the host?"

"He's not rebelling, Bedlam." I addressed the demon, but I watched the archangel. "He wants peace and hope and mercy and light and all those good things that Heaven claims to stand for. He's just not sure that he's been effectively implementing all those values."

Gabriel's eyes widened as he stood up straighter. "You can tell all that just looking at me? You really do have Lucifer's power." *I had heard... but I didn't really believe... I know Michael could be right. She could be evil, especially if she has affection for one of Lucifer's more notorious minions. But if there's even a chance that she isn't, don't we have to take it?*

I tried to put as much sincerity in my words as I could. "I don't know where the power comes from. And I can't speak to its similarity to Lucifer's. I certainly don't have all the answers; I can't tell you anything except what's already inside of you. But if you tell me your story, I will tell you what I see."

Gabriel took a deep breath and began to speak.

CHAPTER 5

"**G**OD CREATED ME AS THE angel of joy, third in the host of Heaven after Lucifer, the angel of glory, and Michael, the angel of order. My primary duty was to spread the news of His love to all of creation. For eons, I excelled at this task."

Gabriel turned to gaze out the window. "When Lucifer chose to rebel, I could not fathom his motivations. I could not understand why so many angels would defy what I could only see as the most wonderful force in the universe. So I fought—not to destroy the adversary, not to defend my way of life, but to try to communicate to the lapsed believer the marvel that is our Creator. I failed."

The sun reflected off Gabriel's blond hair, and I found myself captivated by the glints of gold.

"I don't take all the blame upon myself, of course. After all, to trust in a glorious and omnipotent God, one must also trust that He has a plan, that everything that happens is for the best. I can't know whether He intended the Fall or accepted it. I do know I did all that was in my power to prevent it."

Bedlam rolled his eyes. "Seriously, you too?"

Gabriel frowned at the demon. *I open my heart, and he mocks me?* "What do you mean, me too?"

"I don't get why all the demons—and, apparently, some of the angels—are still obsessed with the war," Bedlam said. "The war is over. It's been over for... for... longer than Khet's been alive! Move on, already."

Gabriel narrowed his eyes at the demon. "But the war matters, Bedlam. Everything goes back to it. One way or another, that rebellion caused the Fall of mankind. It was inevitable that, given free will, some humans would choose to stand beside the fallen angels." He took a deep breath, and his features smoothed over. "But I also knew God would find a way to save these people, so I took joy in knowing someday I would be able to deliver that news."

Gabriel looked straight at me, and the sorrow in his face and mind made my heart ache. "But now that day has come, and I feel more lost than ever before."

He seemed at a loss for how to continue, so I gestured toward a wooden chair at a table next to the window. "Sit down and tell me about it."

Gabriel pulled out the chair and sat. *Where do I begin?* "There is a woman named Mary who lives in the far reaches of this empire. God chose her of all the women in the world to give birth to His son, and He tasked me with informing her of this honor. All I could think was how wonderful it was that I could at last bring tidings of salvation to humanity."

"So, how do you get chosen for something like that?" Bedlam asked. "Being the mother of God, I mean. Is there some kind of heavenly beauty contest?"

I thought Gabriel was going to ignore him—I would have—but he regarded Bedlam seriously. "You know, I have no idea how she was chosen. Michael picked her, I think. Or maybe God did. I just did what they told me to do. I traveled to her town and found a young girl with long brown hair kneeling by her bed. I told her I brought her tidings of great joy, and the Lord had chosen her above all women." Gabriel folded and unfolded his hands on top of the table. "But as I spoke, she became afraid. She tried to run away, so I grabbed her arm to hold her in place. She struggled so much that I realized I was hurting her and let her go."

I wanted to say something to ease the archangel's

distress at the memory, but his blue eyes refused to meet mine. I stood up and walked over to the other chair at the table and sat down. I placed my hands atop Gabriel's shaking fingers. "It's okay. Just tell me what happened."

His lips turned upward as he looked at me, but his eyes remained solemn. "I dematerialized and followed her, anxious to see what had upset her so. She ran into her mother's waiting arms. She told her parents there had been a strange man in her bedroom and he had frightened her. Her parents were dismayed at the red mark my hand had left on her arm, but they could not see me and chose to let the incident pass."

"I think you're making too big a deal about this, Gabs." Bedlam stretched out on the bed I'd vacated. "Scaring humans is half the fun of doing stuff on earth."

I did my best to give him a disapproving look. "Not everyone sees humans as a source of entertainment."

Bedlam stuck his tongue out at me. *Why's she taking his side?*

Gabriel moved his hands to place them atop mine. I was surprised by how much I didn't want him to let them go. "I tried to contact God to ask Him if I was doing what He wanted. He told me I was doing as He desired, but when I asked for further guidance, I received no instruction."

I tried to meet his eyes again, but he was looking away, his eyes resting on a crooked painting hanging on the wall.

"I considered my next actions. I did not want to cause Mary further distress, but I needed to find a way to talk to her on her own. I decided to seek the assistance of Somniel, the angel of peace. That night, she walked through Mary's town, bringing a deep sleep to all the townspeople but Mary."

He pulled his hands away from mine and stood up. He walked over to the painting he had been studying and straightened it. "This time when I appeared to Mary, I allowed her to run away from me. I followed her as she ran into her parents' room and tried to shake them awake, then as she rushed outside into the cold night air. She banged on her neighbors' doors begging for help."

"After she failed to rouse several families, she stopped to listen to me. I told her not to be frightened and explained that God wanted her to be the mother of His only son. She seemed dismayed by the news but agreed that she would do as He asked, so long as I woke their villagers from their unnatural slumber—which, of course, I intended to do anyway."

Gabriel turned a suspicious eye to the other paintings on the wall, daring them to be likewise crooked. "I disappeared but did not leave. I needed to understand why our conversation had gone the way it had. I had always seen myself as an agent of God's goodwill, so I was distressed at having caused a girl such suffering."

"I'm hungry." Never one to sit still for long, Bedlam's edginess had been increasing over the course of Gabriel's tale. "Do you have anything to eat?"

I was about to point out to him that he had only materialized half an hour before at most and could not possibly be hungry yet, but I realized that I didn't know the answer to his question. "I'm not even sure where we are."

"We are in a house I have been using for the last few days while I searched for Cassia," Gabriel said. "The people who live here are out of town for the week."

Bedlam's face lit up. "Gabs, are you squatting in someone's house? That is fabulous!"

Gabriel looked confused. "Of course I asked their permission first, and I offered them compensation."

Bedlam rolled his eyes. "Of course you did. Does that mean that there is or is not food?"

Gabriel pointed. "There is a kitchen through that door."

Bedlam beamed. "I'll be right back."

Gabriel watched the demon go, and then turned to me. "Should I wait for him?"

I shrugged. "He didn't say to. It's hard to tell how much attention he's paying."

"Where was I?" Gabriel crossed and uncrossed his arms. "Right, Mary was upset, and I didn't understand why. Well, she was still unhappy the next day. She dropped things as she performed her household chores and refused to speak with Joseph, the carpenter's son that she was to marry. The next several days passed in a similar manner. Mary's parents were driven to distraction by her erratic behavior, and Joseph could not understand why she refused to see him. Days turned into weeks, and still I watched her, unable to determine why she was so affected by my news."

I kept my eyes focused on Gabriel, but he seemed to want to look at everything in the room but me. His eyes fell on a broom in the corner, and he walked over and picked it up. "During this time, Mary's body began to change. It became more and more apparent that she was carrying a child. She tried to hide it behind her loose clothes, but there came a point at which her parents could no longer pretend they didn't notice." Gabriel swept the mosaic tiles of the floor, his motions increasing in speed as the story continued. "They grew angry with her, and her father hit her and called her a shameless harlot. I expected her to explain my visit to her family. After all, they believed in God. Surely they could understand the miracle that was happening to their child. But she said nothing. She took each physical blow with silent tears and each harsh word with a look of shame."

Tears formed in Gabriel's eyes as he moved the broom across the floor, no longer paying attention to the direction of his strokes. "I thought to appear to them, as well, but Michael had ordered me to tell as few people as possible the true nature of Mary's child. Instead I bore witness as Mary took every blow and insult and watched as she walked through the village, unable to hide the purple swelling on her face. The shameless gossips didn't even have the decency to lower their voices as they laughed at her misfortune, and Joseph no longer sought out her company."

I stood up and walked over to him. I put my hands on the broom to stop his desperate movements.

His red-rimmed eyes met mine. "I couldn't help but think that her suffering was my fault. I had followed God's instructions to the letter, but there had to be some way to fix this. I prayed for enlightenment but received no response."

"Oh, Gabriel." I wanted to reach out and wipe the sorrow off his face. I lifted my hand.

Bedlam came back into the room carrying a tray laden with bread, cheese, and grapes. "They've got a little shrine-thing off the kitchen for their household gods, and they have you, but not me." He sat down in the chair Gabriel had been sitting in earlier.

I dropped my hands from the broom and looked away from Gabriel.

The angel cleared his throat and frowned at the demon. "What are you talking about?"

Bedlam ripped off a hunk of bread and stuffed it into his mouth. "Well, you know how the gods here are based on stories about angels and demons?" Gabriel looked as if he didn't, but given his apparent lack of knowledge about humanity in general, that didn't surprise me. "Anyway, they have Apollo—meaning you—and Minerva-slash-Rachel, but they don't have Mercury. I feel slighted."

Gabriel began sweeping evenly with the broom again. "Wait, if that's true, which angel is Vulcan?" I guess he had more knowledge about Roman religion than I thought.

"I'm not sure." Bedlam furrowed his brow as he considered. "Maybe Mephistopheles? It's not an exact science."

Gabriel shook his head and gave Bedlam a stern look. "Can I finish my story now?"

Bedlam smiled, ignoring the angel's chastisement. "Sure. What'd I miss?"

I moved to sit again in the chair I had vacated. "Mary's parents found out she was pregnant, and they're not happy."

Bedlam popped a grape into his mouth. "Like, no honey cakes after dinner unhappy?"

I reached out and pulled off a grape for myself. "Like beat her and have her shunned by society unhappy."

"That's unfortunate." Bedlam took a knife and began to slice into the cheese. "I miss all the good parts."

"Anyway," Gabriel said, directing our attention back to his story. "I had to do something to help Mary, so I decided to tell her fiancé, Joseph. Mary's parents had canceled the engagement, but I thought I could persuade him to marry her anyway. Based on what the people in town whispered, Mary would be far less dishonored if she had a husband. And even if the townspeople still mocked her, he could take her away from this place, to somewhere that no one knew of her disgrace."

"Sound logic, Gabs." Bedlam offered both Gabriel and me slices of cheese.

I accepted mine, but Gabriel declined. "That night, Joseph was working late in his father's workshop. I tried to greet him as I had Mary, and I knew he would probably be no friendlier to me than Mary had been. But I did not expect him to start throwing his tools at me."

Bedlam's eyes lit up. *Ooh, I bet I can make him jump.* I realized he was going to echo the story and throw his knife at Gabriel. I grabbed his arm and mouthed, "*No.*" Bedlam stuck out his tongue at me, but he retracted his hand and returned to cutting the cheese.

Gabriel was too wrapped up in his story to notice the exchange, which was probably for the best. "As I dodged the hammers and chisels, I explained to Joseph that he needed to marry Mary so she would have a decent life

56

and God's child would be raised in a proper household. Joseph did not believe that God had sent me, and he had nothing but scorn for Mary. But eventually I was able to persuade him that the decent thing to do was give Mary a respectable life, no matter her sins. He promised to treat her well, even though he claimed he could never love her."

Bedlam grinned. "Aw, see, so happy ending after all."

Gabriel sighed. "I don't know that I would call it happy, but I realized that was the most I could ask for. I continued to watch the town for a few days more to ensure that he kept his word. At that point, Michael sought me out. Other plans for the arrival of the Savior were underway, and he wanted me back to help coordinate Heaven's efforts. I explained why I had stayed away longer than I'd anticipated and discovered he was unsurprised by the events I had witnessed."

Bedlam and I exchanged glances. *Oh, here we go,* he thought. We both knew that the appearance of Michael in the story was not going to lead to anything good.

Gabriel clenched the broom in his hand until his knuckles turned white. "Michael told me this kind of behavior, this lack of faith, was why mankind needed to be saved. He said that the suffering of one girl or one town meant nothing when the result was the release of generations of souls from eternal damnation. People would remember that a virgin had given birth to a son, and the details wouldn't matter. Michael had been my friend and leader since the beginning of time, and I realized that I did not understand him nearly so well as I thought I had."

Gabriel's shoulders slumped as his anger gave way to despair. "Or maybe it was the world that I did not understand. Or maybe it was myself. All I wanted—all I ever wanted—was to spread the joy of the news of God's love to all of creation. I could not see any joy in what I did there."

Gabriel avoided meeting my gaze as he returned the

broom to its place in the corner. "I remembered a time once, long ago, before the Fall, when Lucifer had been our leader. He could see how we fit into God's plan and always knew how to reassure us that we were on the right path or redirect us when we strayed. I needed that insight again."

He turned and walked closer to me, his eyes still studying the mosaic on the floor. "I could not go to Lucifer, of course, but I remembered hearing about a girl, a human girl, who had been born with his power. I knew I must tell her my story and seek her guidance." He fell to his knees in front of me and looked at me with wide, earnest eyes. "And so I beg you. Tell me how I can fix this misery I have wrought."

"I cannot." I wanted nothing more than to give him a simple answer, but there was none to be had. "You want me to tell you that doing what God commands is always correct or to find some way to make Mary's pain acceptable to you, but... I cannot. I can only tell you what I see in you, that your soul burns with a greater desire to do good than any I have ever seen."

"Wait, Khet. I think you can actually help!" Bedlam twirled the knife around in his fingers. *Poor Gabs. He's just trying to do good in his clueless idiot way. Too bad there's no room for that in a Michael plan. And those poor people in the story! I hope I didn't lead any demons or psycho-killers to them.*

"I don't really see how, Bedlam." I felt a wave of sadness wash over me. "I'm sorry that this plan of Heaven's is causing so much pain, but I can't do anything about it. Plus, I think in this case Michael is right, and the good outweighs the harm."

Bedlam snorted. "I could go into a long diatribe about how much I categorically disagree with the notion of Michael ever being right, but even I recognize that this would most likely cause an irrelevant argument that would prevent me from ever getting my point across. Anyway, I'm not suggesting that we undo everything, because we can't. But we can help Mary and Joseph!"

Gabriel's brow furrowed. "We can?"

"Absolutely!" Bedlam bounced up and down at the prospect. "I mean, the whole problem here is that no one believes Gabs. But Khet can see into everyone's heads and see what they need to hear to believe that the baby does come from God. It's a perfect plan!"

"That actually might work," said Gabriel.

I considered this plan for a moment. "Well, I don't know that I should tell everyone. After all, it's probably for the best that too many people don't know who the baby is. But I could at least try to help Mary and Joseph."

"Hurrah!" Bedlam jumped up. "Let's go to Bethlehem!"

Gabriel eyed the demon. "I don't know that you should come, Bedlam. Michael is sure to react badly if he sees you near the child. And..." *And I don't trust you.*

Bedlam laughed and stuck his tongue out at the archangel. "Don't be a spoilsport, Gabs! I wouldn't miss this for the world! And I'll be on my best behavior. I won't cause any riots or create any sandstorms or start any new religions or anything!"

The trip took longer than we expected. Bedlam kept insisting we stop and see a crucifixion or the world's longest aqueduct. But after several weeks' travel, Gabriel led us to the small house where Mary, Joseph, and the baby Jesus dwelt. I knocked on the door, and a girl who looked far too young to carry the fate of the world in her womb opened it. I made an amused sound in my throat. I too knew what it was like to be far too young to have a horrible destiny. Mary seemed to handle it with more aplomb than I did, at least, since she was still living in a town and caring for a baby, as evidenced by the bit of spittle dried on the shoulder of her tunic.

Mary's eyes widened when she saw Gabriel, and she took a step back. "It's all right." I reached out to give her arm a reassuring squeeze. "We aren't here to hurt you."

I glanced around the room as I stepped inside. Despite the warm fire burning in the hearth, I could feel a chill in the air. To the side of the room, I saw a man with specks of sawdust in his beard, who I assumed must be Joseph. The wall of mistrust between him and Mary was so thick that I could almost reach out and touch it. He looked up when Gabriel entered the room, and I was surprised to feel a spark of hope from him. On some level, he knew that what Gabriel had said to him was true, and he wanted someone to convince him of it.

Mary sat in a well-made wooden chair, and I knelt down beside her. "Mary, you know what happened to you, even if no one else does. I know it seems like it has ruined your life, but you have to know that God placed this burden on you because you are special. He knows that you can withstand it in order to make everything better for humanity."

Mary nodded with tears in her eyes. *At last someone else knows the truth.*

"And Joseph." I turned to Mary's husband. "You know in your heart that Mary is a good woman, that she would never lie to you or betray you. What can I do to make you believe it?" I looked into his mind and let out an audible laugh.

Gabriel looked puzzled. "What is it?"

"He thinks that you should glow."

Joseph's cheeks reddened as he looked down at his lap. "Angels are supposed to have halos."

I looked at Gabriel and expected to have some explanation why he couldn't oblige. Instead, I gasped as a yellow light suffused the air all around the angel, as if his inner radiance were now visible for everyone to see. The glow washed away Mary and Joseph's doubts, and I found that I too could believe in the glory of angels—or, at least, of one angel.

"Oh, Mary." Joseph stood up and walked over to his

wife. He knelt down and embraced her. "I'm sorry I didn't believe you. It was all just so..."

"It's all right." Tears sprang to Mary's eyes. "I understand why you thought what you did. The whole situation was hard to believe."

Joseph glanced at Gabriel and me. "But what does this mean for the child?"

I had no idea what to tell them, and was grateful when Gabriel smiled. "It means he has a great future ahead of him, and he will need all your love and care to be ready for it."

Gabriel and I left soon thereafter, and as soon as we stepped out in the open air, he took my hand. "I can't thank you for what you've done for me. What you gave to Mary and Joseph—it was more than anyone in Heaven was willing to give."

I felt the heat rising to my cheeks. "I'm sure they would have, given time. They're busy with other things, right now." That wasn't true, and I knew it. In my experience, most of the angels in Heaven weren't interested in anything but their own self-righteous opinions. But I couldn't bring myself to say that to the being in front of me.

He shook his head. "No. I have done more good in this last hour than I have done in thousands of years in Heaven. I'm not going back to that. There must be any number of things I can do down here. With you."

I looked up into his blue eyes and found I couldn't tell what he was thinking. "That's..."

Bedlam appeared next to us.

"Where have you been?" Gabriel asked.

Bedlam scowled. "Nowhere." He looked at me and brightened. "So are we leaving yet? I heard a rumor that the next village over has a two-headed goat. We have to check it out!"

Bedlam thought that our road trip was what inspired the tale of the three wise men, even though we came from the west. Every year he came up with some new theory of which of us carried gold, frankincense, or myrrh. Some years it was just the two of us celebrating Christmas together, and some years Gabriel joined us, but every year we laughed at his interpretations of wealth of gold as Gabriel's hair or Bedlam's panache, the sacred frankincense as Gabriel's holiness or my healing powers, and the bitter omen of myrrh as Bedlam's fall or my curse. But inside, we were all also a little sad, because each of us believed that we were the one who carried the myrrh.

CHAPTER 6

"**Y**OU SENT HIM?" BEDLAM EXCLAIMED at Gabriel as the angel sat down at the counter a few stools away from the demon.

Gabriel's brow furrowed. "No, I sent a girl whose brother had exchanged his soul for her life. I thought Cassia could help her accept it."

"You idiot!" For a moment I thought Bedlam was going to smack the blond angel. "What were you thinking? Didn't it occur to you that she might not be seeking help for herself? She must have gone and told her brother where to find Khet!"

I should have come to my own defense as well, but whenever I first encountered Gabriel after a long time away, I was struck dumb by the radiant light and warmth of his presence. The humiliating truth was that I loved him more than I could say. And though it was possible for an angel to love a human, I had never once in two thousand years of searching his soul found any evidence that Gabriel saw me as anything more than a friend.

Realization dawned on Gabriel's face. "Someone with a demonic contract came to see Cassia?"

Bedlam made a disgusted noise. "Yeah, and she's been in a funk about it all week. I can't believe you sent him! Even I know better than that."

I waved my hand. "I'm right here, guys!"

Gabriel's cheeks colored. "It never occurred to me that she might send her brother here. She was so sad."

"It's fine, Gabriel." I did my best to sound like the mature eight thousand-year-old woman that I was and not the giggling schoolgirl I feared I resembled.

"It is not fine!" Bedlam narrowed his eyes at me. "You don't have to help everyone."

"There's nothing wrong with helping people," Gabriel said. *Why is he always so selfish?*

"Not in theory." Bedlam responded to Gabriel's statement but directed his words at me. "But when you spend all your time trying to solve an inherently unsolvable problem—like, say, making it okay that someone sold his soul—you aren't so much helping as repeatedly banging your head against a wall. Or should we tell Gabs about the woman last year who didn't want social services to take her children away but refused to give up her heroin habit? Or how about the kid who had to drop out of college and get a job to take care of his brothers, after his parents died in the car crash? Oh, and let's not forget the guy who beat his daughter into a coma when he found out she'd had an abortion after she was raped."

"You're right." He was. In every one of those cases I had gone out of my way to help someone only to have everything blow up in my face, and Bedlam had been the one to pick up the pieces. I could try to point out the numerous cases where I had succeeded in helping people, but any attempts to solve Sebastian's problems would end in disappointment.

Bedlam took a swig out of his coffee mug. "That would be more comforting if I thought you had any intention of not sticking your neck out to help whatever poor slob shows up next."

He was right about that too, but I didn't see any point in discussing it. "Gabriel, would you like something to eat?"

He glanced over at the tomato seeds and marshmallow goop left on Bedlam's plate, which was enough to spoil anyone's appetite. "No, thanks, Cassia. I'm good for now."

"You know what your problem is, Gabs?" Bedlam made an excessive show of consuming the last large bite of his meal. "You have no sense of adventure."

"Really?" Gabriel said. "I've spent the last month in a monsoon-stricken part of the Pacific, which I would think would be adventurous enough even for you."

Bedlam brightened. "I was telling Khet that we should check out the monsoons!" He turned to me, "See, Khet? Even Gabriel likes the monsoons. It's not some crazy obsession of mine!"

"I'm fairly certain that Gabriel was there to assist the victims, not because he finds crashing tidal waves satisfying to watch." I turned my attention back to Gabriel. "So if the monsoons are still around, what brings you to Philadelphia?"

"Well, most of the emergency work was done, and I ran into that girl I sent to you, who was also aiding the monsoon victims. And then I realized it had been a while since I had stopped by to see you, so I thought I'd come here. I think I will volunteer at one of the free clinics awhile, and Philabundance can always use a few helping hands. I should be in town for a few months, at least."

I smiled, unable to disguise my delight. I couldn't remember the last time he had stuck around so long. The promise of three months of Gabriel's company was almost enough to make me forget about Sebastian.

One morning a week or so after Gabriel's arrival, I found myself alone in the diner with Bedlam. He was eating pickles, bologna, and gummy bears, with a garlic-flavored English muffin. He had been so anxious to try out this new combination that he went out to purchase the gummy bears himself, as they were not anywhere on the diner's menu.

I was still the one paying for the candy. I had decided a long time ago that it was in the best interests of the world at large if Bedlam had access to all my financial resources. I have the kind of wealth that one can only achieve through several lifetimes of savings, and if I didn't share with Bedlam, he would no doubt find other, less savory ways to obtain whatever he wanted. I worried that he would someday find a way to bankrupt me, but he had yet to come even close.

I had finished picking up a few stray gummy bears—white ones; Bedlam felt the pineapple didn't go with the rest of the flavors—when I felt a radiant presence enter the diner. I smiled as I looked up, expecting to see Gabriel, even though he had said that he likely wouldn't be by until later that day. Yet when I met the eyes of my new guest, I was surprised to see the other man who had been occupying my thoughts of late: Sebastian.

"Hey, it's you again." Bedlam's open mouth revealed a confetti of a shocking variety of colors and consistencies. He chewed and swallowed before holding out his hand. "I'm Bedlam."

I narrowed my eyes at the demon. He seemed genuinely pleased to see Sebastian, and I could not believe that he had forgotten his disapproval of the man. But all I got from his mind was *The texture of these gummy bears goes great with the garlic.*

The young man shook the demon's hand, seeming puzzled at the exuberant greeting from a complete stranger. "Hello, I'm Sebastian. Do you—?"

"Seriously? Sebastian? Did your parents hate you?"

I shook my head. Bedlam was only curious and not trying to be rude, but most people did not pick up on that nuance. "You can ignore Bedlam if you want. Most people do."

Bedlam stuck his food-flecked tongue out at me before continuing to eat his sandwich.

"No, that's all right." Sebastian sat down and glanced at the demon to his left. "Though I think that 'Bedlam' is a far stranger name than 'Sebastian.' You were named after the forces of chaos?"

Bedlam grinned. "Nope. The forces of chaos were named after me."

Sebastian's brow furrowed. "I thought the word 'Bedlam' came from the nickname of the Bethlehem Asylum in London."

"That's what they want you to think." Bedlam took a bite out of his sandwich. "My real name is Azazel, but the only person who calls me that is Luci. And that's mostly to irritate me."

"Your parents named you after a demon?"

"Not exactly."

Sebastian laughed nervously. *This person sitting next to me is crazy, possibly in a violent way. And his eyes. There's something... wrong about them. They remind me of...* He edged his stool a few centimeters to the right. "Oh, okay. Well, my parents named all their children after martyrs. My sister is Felicity, and my brother is Stephen."

"Huh." Bedlam wrinkled his nose. "Well, if they brought you up to admire that kind of behavior, it's no wonder you ended up selling your soul to Azrael."

Sebastian's mouth dropped open. "How did you...?" He broke off as he came to the logical, if erroneous, conclusion. "You're the Oracle!"

Bedlam laughed. "Me? No way!" He pointed at me. "She's the Oracle. I just hang out here for the free food."

Sebastian turned his attention to me, and I nodded. "I'm Carrie."

I had begun clearing up the ingredients for Bedlam's food as they talked, and now I focused on using a twist tie to seal the English muffins rather than look at the man who now knew I had been less than honest with him on his previous visit.

Then why didn't she tell me when I came in before? His thought betrayed his irritation, but he didn't let it show in his voice. "It's okay. I don't actually expect anyone to be able to help me. Some man told my sister that there was an oracle here. I didn't want to come, but the girl can be relentless. When she found out I didn't follow her instructions and order something, she sent me back. I guess I was supposed to talk to you and not that other woman." He glanced back at Madame Zarita's booth, which was empty today. The psychic was spending the day with her grandchildren.

"Yes, your sister talked to my friend Gabriel. When he meets someone who he thinks can use my help, he gives them those instructions." I paused, unsure of what to say next. He said that he didn't expect anyone to be able to help him, but that wasn't exactly true. He still had some hope that I could help him, or else he wouldn't have come. "I'm not sure what I'll be able to do for you. But maybe if you tell me your story, I can come up with something." *Offering the poor boy false hope? What is wrong with you, Carrie? You know you can't do anything to help him.*

I spared a glance at Bedlam, who had narrowed his eyes at me. He was starting to regret welcoming Sebastian instead of removing him from my presence. *I know that look. That's the look that says "I'm about to do something colossally stupid in the name of 'the greater good.'"*

"There's not that much to tell. When my sister was about thirteen, she was diagnosed with leukemia. It was a very stressful time for the whole family." His words were stoic, but underneath them was a current of raw emotion so strong that I had to grip my hands against the counter to keep steady. "Eventually she achieved a remission, but it was a near thing. Then about three years ago, during her senior year of high school, the remission ended, and she got sick again. The doctors kept saying that we had to be positive, that she had fought it once and could do so again. But we knew that there really wasn't any hope."

"It's not like my sister was perfect or anything. I mean,

she was a teenage girl, so she could be catty. And as I said before, if she wants you to do something, she will hound you until you either do it or go mad. But she's loyal to her friends, and she loves her family. She had already decided that she wanted to become a doctor and try to find a cure for leukemia—'to help kids like me,' she said. She had been granted early admission to Penn's pre-med program, and she was looking forward to having an exciting senior year."

"When the cancer came back, it was like all the light and hope went out of her. She put on a brave face for our parents, but I know she cried every night she spent in the hospital. She was in so much pain, and the medicine was making her feel almost as bad. I couldn't bear to see her suffer any longer."

"So let me guess." I had been so wrapped up in Sebastian's story that I had to remind myself to breathe, but Bedlam's sarcastic tone suggested that he was less than impressed. "You went down by the river and declared to all the powers of the universe that you would do anything if you could save the sister that you loved so much."

"Um... Actually, yes." *Wow. That's a surprisingly on-target guess.*

But, of course, it wasn't a guess. "And then, lo and behold, what should happen, but the most beautiful woman you had ever seen appeared before you. She smiled at you and told you that she could save your sister. And you might have thought that she was an angel answering your prayers, except that her eyes were black and cold as the darkest corners of your soul, the ones that you try to pretend to yourself don't exist but that have a habit of creeping up on you when you are all alone in the middle of the night."

Sebastian shuddered at Bedlam's words. *He's one of them. Like Azrael.*

"She told you that she would help your sister for you, and all you would have to do is give her your soul. She would even let you have three more years to spend with your sister before coming to collect."

"Almost word for word." Sebastian appeared shaken for another moment, but then I felt a conviction solid as a steel plate rise in his mind. "But I didn't even need a minute to consider her offer. I spelled out the terms of the agreement very strictly, that Felicity was to be cured from her cancer—a real cure, not just remission—and none of the powers of Hell were allowed to interfere with the rest of her natural life. Then we both cut our hands and sealed our pact with blood."

Bedlam rolled his eyes and popped the last bite of his sandwich into his mouth. "Did that seriously seem strict to you? 'Natural life' has all kinds of wiggle room. Her natural life was supposed to end with her dying of leukemia."

"Bedlam, be nice," I said, though I had little expectation that he would.

Bedlam didn't even spare me a glance. "And at what point did you realize this was a bad idea? When you woke up the next morning and discovered that your hand was now marked with the symbol of Azrael? Or was it the realization that time was slowly running out?"

"Neither. He's not sorry he did it." I saw in his mind that he was as certain of his decision to sell his soul as he had been the day he made it. "Except he wishes that his sister hadn't found out."

Sebastian nodded once. "Everyone else—our parents and brother, Felicity's friends, the doctors—were all willing to accept that it was a miracle. But Felicity had been through the recovery process before, and she knew something was different this time. She noticed that I did not seem as surprised by her recovery as everyone else, and she spotted the brand on my hand. I don't know how she found out what it meant. Maybe she found an old book or a website, or talked to a priest who still believes in demons. But she did find out, and she was not happy.

She doesn't understand that I did the right thing, and I'm not sorry."

His sister tells him he made the wrong choice, and he still doesn't believe it, I thought. *Stubborn. I knew there had to be a fault in there somewhere.*

Bedlam opened his mouth to interject something, but I silenced him with a small shake of my head. I knew what he wanted to say, because on some level I was thinking the same thing. Sebastian was playing with forces he could not possibly understand. Hell always came out ahead in those games. After a short time in Hell, he would be sorry that he had traded his eternal existence for something as brief as his sister's life.

But I couldn't tell Sebastian that. All he had was his conviction that he had done the right thing, and I couldn't take that away from him. If all I could give him were a few more days of that certainty, that was what I was going to do.

"Thank you for telling me your story. I'm sorry that I can't do anything to help you. If you would like, you can send your sister to see me. I will tell her that you don't regret what you chose. I can try to make her understand."

"Thank you for that." Sebastian smiled at me, and I realized that the knowledge that his sister would have someone with whom to talk had eased a burden for him. "You know, I actually do feel better, having told someone about all this. At least someone will understand what I did when I'm gone."

"Well, I can promise you that I will remember you for the rest of my life. Now, is there anything I can get you?"

He shook his head. "Well, I did promise Felicity that I would order something this time. But, if it's all the same to you, I think she will agree that I have achieved what she intended, and I'm not all that hungry." *Plus, I checked out the reviews for this place. No thank you.*

"Well, here, take some coffee for the road, at least. On

the house." I filled a paper cup from the pot and stopped the tendrils of steam rising from it by snapping on a plastic lid. I forced a smile onto my face as I handed it to him. "You wouldn't want to have to tell Felicity that you disregarded her instructions a second time."

He thanked me and left the diner, somehow with a lighter spirit than when he arrived. My heart, however, was back to being as heavy as it was when he had stopped by nearly two weeks ago. In spite of all my years and alleged powers to soothe people's hearts and souls, there was nothing that I could do to right this wrong. I didn't know why God allowed such a thing to happen—why He allowed Azrael to win in this situation.

And I realized that, more than anything in the world, I wanted to save that poor, good boy's soul.

CHAPTER 7

THE DISHWASHER IN THE DINER was on the fritz, so I found myself with a pile of dishes in even worse shape than could be excused by my diner's reputation. So I put on a pair of yellow rubber gloves, hauled a pile of plates and bowls to the sink behind the counter, and prepared myself for an afternoon of scouring by hand.

As always when there is work to be done, Bedlam had gone off to do whatever it was that he did. He told me tales of his adventures, of course, but it was difficult even for me to tell what he was making up and what he was exaggerating. Mostly, he went out and watched people or granted random wishes that he overheard them making. Every so often he did something really bizarre, like help an elephant escape from a local zoo, to see what would happen. And one time he made every snowflake in a Detroit blizzard identical, though I don't think that anyone noticed.

As I washed the dishes, I considered ways that I could make contact with Azrael. *Not that I'm going to do that,* I thought as I scrubbed at a stubborn yolk stain. *Not that I even could. Sebastian may have stood by a river to call her, but that wouldn't work for me. Azrael doesn't visit everyone who stands by a river and wishes to save someone they love. Besides, I don't love Sebastian.*

I rinsed the plate and set it in the drying rack. *And even if I find Azrael, I can't make her give up his soul. It's hers, fair and square. Unless I found something she wanted more. Maybe if I looked into her mind...*

I made a face as I grabbed the next mug and realized that some diner had left an unrecognizable, foul-smelling slimy sludge at the bottom of it. *But it's stupid to try and think of what I would do in her presence when I don't know how to find her. Which doesn't matter anyway, because I am* not *going to save Sebastian's soul.*

At this point in my musings, I felt someone enter the diner. The intensity of the soul marked it as an angel, and the feelings of contempt and desperation that joined my emotions in my head could only belong to one of my least favorite people in all of earth, Heaven, or Hell.

I looked over my shoulder and, sure enough, found myself in the presence of a tall woman with sharp features and long brown hair, the bangs of which just avoided falling into her blue eyes. Even though her green dress made her look like she should be serving drinks at a Renaissance Faire, she gazed down her aquiline nose at me and put a great deal of effort into making sure I knew that every fiber of her being felt nothing but disdain for my existence. In fact, I was so unimportant that she did not feel the need to obey Michael's command that she never come near me again.

"Hello, Keziel." I pulled my hands out of the lemon-scented water and shook some of the suds off them. "Bedlam isn't here."

Keziel only came to see me for one reason. She always had some other pretext for coming—sometimes with excuses that were even as urgent as she made them seem—but, in reality, they were still rationalizations for the fact that she yearned for Bedlam's company.

Angels liked to talk about the differences between themselves and humans, but they had a number of similarities, as well. Angels were as capable of falling in love as humans, and when they were in human form, they could experience love in all the same ways. Where they differed from humans, in what some might say was their

74

biggest design flaw, was that they could not fall out of love.

That should have led to a bunch of happy angel couples, but for the most part, the opposite was true, and angels ended up eternally miserable in love. All kinds of desires and obligations could create problems between two people, and sometimes these problems became insurmountable. When that happened to humans, they could separate and go on with their lives. When it happened to angels, they got caught in a horrible state wherein they didn't want to be with someone, but they couldn't stop loving them, and they couldn't fall in love with someone else. Such was the case with Keziel and Bedlam.

I didn't know all the details of their tragic story. Bedlam didn't like to talk about it. I could only gather so much from the more-bitter-than-sweet memories in his head, and Keziel had never offered to tell me her version.

What I do know is Keziel, the fourth highest angel in the hierarchy, the angel of nature and balance, was tasked with creating the world; Bedlam and Jophiel, the angel of service, assisted her. During that time, Keziel and Bedlam fell in love, possibly the first couple to ever do so.

After the world was made, Keziel wanted to thank the angels who had aided her, so she offered to grant each of them any wish within her power. Jophiel asked that Keziel stand beside him forever and use her power to serve the wishes of Heaven. Keziel did not wish to comply with Jophiel's request, but she said that, as an angel, she had to keep her word and grant his wish, despite Bedlam's pleas. And so Keziel not only invented marriage but also became the first woman ever to choose to marry for security instead of love.

Bedlam did not take the loss of Keziel well, and I don't think I would have liked to see him in those days. When Lucifer started his rebellion, the angel of chaos was one of the first to join up, as well as one of the most vehement fighters. I think he was even a bit relieved when he got kicked out of Heaven.

He had allowed himself to live in the hole that she left in his life until the incident that brought him to me shocked him back into reality. He still had a lot of bitterness, but he liked nothing better than to watch a hurricane or tornado, nature and chaos working together toward a common but doomed goal.

"I'm not here to see Bedlam." Keziel put her hands on her hips in a remarkable, if unintentional, Wonder Woman impression. "Unlike some people, I have no interest in associating with demons."

That's a lie, she thought. *She knows it, with her creepy power. I hate that she, of all people, knows that I am so attached to a demon.*

I thought about telling her that I was not the only person who knew she was in love with Bedlam—everyone knew it. But I decided, not for the first time, to be discreet. "Well, I know you can't be here to see me."

I pulled off my rubber gloves and placed them on the counter next to the sink, then turned around to face her. "I seem to recall making it quite clear to both you and Michael that I would not tolerate your presence."

"I have important business with Gabriel." She bristled. "I don't know why he chooses to associate with you, but as long as he does, you will have to accept that I am going to put matters of celestial importance ahead of your trivial feelings."

I held back a groan. I wanted to resent her, but her hostility sprung from jealousy over the time I spent with Bedlam. She didn't have to bother. If she gave Bedlam the choice, he would have far preferred to spend all his time with her.

Besides, underneath her petulant hostility lay real fear. *Something's going to happen. I can feel it in the wind through my hair and the ground under my toes. Something big is going to happen that is going to change the balance, and I need Bedlam— No, I need Gabriel. I need Gabriel to come back to Heaven and do his job.*

"Gabriel isn't here either." I tried to make my tone gentler and reached out my hand to give hers a sympathetic pat. "But if you give me a message, I'll make sure that he gets it."

Keziel pulled her hand away and looked at me as if I were a carrier of some kind of angel leprosy. "As if I would entrust a message for Gabriel to you! It's your fault he's down here in the first place, instead of working toward the greater good in Heaven where he belongs."

I sighed. I couldn't say that she was wrong, though I doubted I had as much of a hold on Gabriel as she seemed to think. "Well, Keziel, you have two choices. You can either leave the message for Gabriel with me and then go away, or you can just go away. But you cannot stay here, and I will call Michael if I have to."

That was a bluff. I didn't want to call Michael, but Keziel did not possess anything like my gift for understanding people's motivations.

"Fine," she said in a voice that I would've described as a sulk in anyone who wasn't an angel. "I'll go. But tell him that I was here looking for him, and don't blame me if his failure to hear my message leads to ruin."

Without another word, she disappeared. Angels did have a flair for the melodramatic.

Keziel's visit unnerved me a bit, but if anything serious occurred, Michael would come banging at my door himself. Besides, whatever happened wouldn't impact me, chained as I was to the earth in the same way sold souls were bound to Hell.

Though, now that I thought about it, that wasn't strictly true. I did know how to get to Hell...

Around the year 1700, Bedlam and I lived in Paris. I worked in a bakery and kept a two-story apartment a few blocks north. We sat at the table in my parlor that looked out on the street, playing backgammon for what seemed the millionth time. We had read all the books on the shelves lining the opposite wall. Bedlam had run out of room on the front of the shelves to put the figurines and creepy dolls he had brought back from around the world, so they were starting to grace the edges of the white sweeping staircase.

I knew I should move on soon, but I wasn't sure where I wanted to go. I didn't think a single change of location would satisfy Bedlam, anyway. He wanted to go on a world tour, and though transportation was improving, I wasn't eager to travel long distances in areas where propriety demanded corsets, hoop skirts, and other unmanageable attire. Bedlam might have been able to make his stylish-but-ridiculous looking coats and wigs appear on a whim, but I actually had to deal with the mechanics of fashion.

"I wish you could teleport, Khet." He rolled the dice and barely took time to consider the pieces before moving two of them. "Then we could go anywhere we wanted. There's a really good tsunami in Japan right now, but there's not really a good way to get there, unless you want to walk across Asia again. And by the time we arrived, the good parts would be done."

I considered once again informing him that I did not share his fondness for natural disasters, since I enjoyed neither the suffering of the victims nor his inevitable bemoaning of his loss of Keziel. But I knew better than to bring her up around him, and there was no point in identifying another obstacle when the ones he mentioned were already insurmountable.

"Sorry." I picked up the dice and placed them in the cup. "Humans only have the one form. No dematerializing for me."

Bedlam narrowed his black eyes at me as I shook the cylinder. "That's being defeatist. I mean, have you ever *tried* to teleport? How can you know that you can't if you never tried?"

I poured the dice onto the board and considered my moves. "I'm sure that someone has tried. Besides, isn't it instinctive to angels? Or did you go through a period in your history where you couldn't teleport, either?"

"Well, angels are different." Even though I wasn't finished with my turn, Bedlam scooped up the dice and dropped them into his cup. "We start out non-corporeal and then can choose to manifest ourselves physically. So maybe that makes it easier." His eyes suddenly lit up. "I know! How about I tell you how I do it and you can try?"

"All right." I didn't really expect it to work, but I thought it would be more interesting than listening to him whine through another game of backgammon.

"Yay!" Bedlam dropped the dice cup onto the board, displacing some of the checkers, and jumped up from his chair.

"Don't you want to finish the game first?"

Bedlam glared at the game table. "No. You're going to win like always."

"You would win if you paid attention." I began to rearrange the pieces on the board so they would be in the proper position for starting a new game.

Bedlam grabbed my hand and turned me away from the table. "Worry about that later. Teleporting now. How do I describe it?" He scrunched up his face in an over-exaggerated display of thought. "So you have to sort of think of your body as a million different particles that are only connected by chance..."

He spent the entire afternoon coming up with metaphors for the process of dematerialization, but no matter how hard I pictured my cells breaking apart or my skin dissolving into the floor, I remained determinedly solid. I expected Bedlam to get frustrated and give up at any moment, but he seemed resolute in his quest to defeat the limits of my human body. He kept teleporting around the room, trying to analyze the nuances of the action.

"Okay, try this!" he said, about three hours after we had begun. "Make your body really, really heavy. And then make everything that isn't your body really, really light."

I closed my eyes and tried not to sigh too loudly as I attempted this latest set of instructions. I didn't really expect anything to happen, but as I sunk into the chair and tried to raise my mind as high as possible, I felt what I can only describe as a full-body *whoosh* at the same time that I heard the *thump* of something falling to the floor. I looked down to see that my body had fallen off the chair, and I was apparently looking at it from the outside

"Khet!" Bedlam rushed to kneel down beside my body. "Khet? Are you all right?"

I felt strange, and not just because I was looking at something I had previously only been able to see in the mirror. I saw and heard everything that was going on around me: Bedlam shaking my shoulders, the clip-clop of horses on the street, the calico cat grooming itself in the corner of the room. I felt the draft coming in from the window. But I couldn't use my power, not in the way I usually could. Bedlam's heart and mind were completely closed to me, and I couldn't discern the presence of souls from the other side of the window. It was peaceful to be alone in my own head.

"*Khet!*"

Well, except for the fact that I wasn't actually in my head, and the alarmed demon in front of me was growing rather loud. I decided that I had better attempt to get back in my body before he panicked. I envisioned my mind becoming heavy again.

I opened my eyes. Bedlam's face was right in front of mine, and he was anxious that he had killed or otherwise permanently damaged me. A bruise was forming on my head where it had made contact with the floor, and I felt pain in my side, where my stays were digging in. "I... I think I did it," I told him, coughing a little as I became re-accustomed to my body.

"Wraith pox, Khet!" he exclaimed. "I don't know what you think happened, but you definitely didn't dematerialize. You fell down. I thought you were dead!"

"No, but I did!" I sat up on the floor, not the easiest process in a hoop skirt. "At least, I managed to separate from my body. I could see it and you and everything."

"Really? I guess that means you can't teleport, after all." He looked disappointed for a moment but then brightened. "But we can totally do other things with this! Let's practice!"

Before I left my body the second time, I removed my hooped underskirt and made sure to be lying on the ground, so that I wouldn't hurt myself. I also stayed out of it for longer so that I could take a better look around me. When Bedlam started to get restless, I returned to my body. "It's so quiet," I told him. "It's nice to only hear myself for a little while. But what's the black, smoky spot over there?" I pointed to an empty patch of carpet toward the side of the room where, in my spirit form, I saw a churning miasma of dark mist.

"You can see that?" he asked, surprised. "That's a hellhole. There are a bunch of them all over the place. You can go through them to get to Hell. You know, if you wanted to go to Hell. Which, why would you, really? Can you see the pearly gates too?"

"Um... I don't know. What's a pearly gate?"

"It's the opposite of a hellhole, a portal to Heaven. They look the same, except that they're that shiny white color and on the ceiling. I used to be able to see them." Bedlam rarely allowed himself to regret his fall, but on that occasion, he spent a few minutes gazing wistfully toward an imagined patch of white smoke in the air above his head.

We spent the next few hours experimenting with my spirit form. We discovered that my ability to read souls worked on anyone who was in the same state as me. If

81

Bedlam dematerialized while I was in spirit form, I could suddenly feel his emotions the same as I could when we were both in human form. We determined that my spirit form could teleport in the same way that Bedlam's could, so long as I didn't mind leaving my body behind. Even moving through space normally, my spirit form moved much more quickly than my body could walk.

We decided that I probably couldn't see the pearly gates, since I couldn't find any in the house, though we couldn't be sure. Bedlam was quite concerned that my failure to see any smoky opalescent spots meant that my soul was damned, but it didn't really make a difference to me. There was no point worrying about what would happen to my soul after my death, since I was never going to die.

We played for a few hours until I felt a burst of sunlight that couldn't be natural that late in the afternoon. I recognized it as my favorite presence and was thrilled when Gabriel materialized in front of me. Bedlam shifted out of spirit form and stood in front of my empty body before Gabriel could become too distracted by it.

"Gabs!" Bedlam exclaimed. "Quick, go into the other room and write something on the paper on Khet's desk. Then leave it there and come back!"

Gabriel looked puzzled but did as he was instructed. When the angel had left the room, Bedlam motioned for me to follow. I floated over and watched Gabriel write, then flew back and landed inside my body relatively smoothly. As Gabriel reentered the room, Bedlam announced in a theatrical tone, "And now the amazing Khet shall divine what our guest has written."

I sat up and giggled as much at Gabriel's bewildered face as at Bedlam's theatrics. "Sadly, it's not that exciting. He wrote 'Hello, my name is Gabriel.'"

"Ach! Boring! The audience is not entertained!"

Gabriel's brow furrowed. "The audience seems plenty entertained. Do I even want to ask what you are doing?"

Bedlam flopped down on the ground next to me. "Well, I've always kind of thought that the fact that humans can't teleport is a major design flaw, but then I thought that maybe that was because no one had ever bothered to teach them—"

"Which, it turns out, is not the real reason—" I interjected.

"Right, humans totally can't move their bodies around. But! It turns out that if Khet tries to dematerialize, she can separate her spirit from her body! So we've been trying it out—"

"You've been doing what?" Gabriel's blue eyes were wide. *Light take me. They're going to kill her.* "What were you thinking?"

Bedlam and I exchanged glances. "Well, we thought—"

Gabriel waved a hand, silencing the demon. "I don't really want to know. What I meant was that clearly, you weren't thinking. Of course humans can separate their souls from their bodies—when they're dead!"

We exchanged another more serious glance. "Oh, I guess I hadn't thought about it that way," I said.

"It's not like she can die anyway," Bedlam muttered. *I should have realized that when she could see the hellholes. Light of Lucifer, why do I never think?*

"Just because she can't die doesn't mean she can't get trapped outside her body or end up in some kind of eternal sleep." Gabriel wouldn't have continued berating the demon if he'd known what Bedlam was thinking. "Cassia. Please. Promise me you'll never do anything like that again."

I looked into his blue eyes and felt tears build up in mine. Even seventeen hundred years after we met, he was still the most beautiful thing I had ever seen. I hated to make him worry about me, especially for something so stupid. "Okay," I said. "I promise."

I kept my promise. I hadn't separated my soul from my body again since that day. Thinking of it now, though, it occurred to me that traveling through a hellhole might be an easy way of reaching Azrael, were I still inclined to talk to her about Sebastian. And there wasn't a reason for me to not intervene on his behalf, if all I had to do was separate from my body and have one conversation with an unpleasant archdemon. And there were a hundred reasons why I should.

I had been focused on the fact that I couldn't find Azrael on earth, but there was no reason that I could not go to Hell and seek her out. Granted, I had never passed through a hellhole, and I had no way of being certain that I would be able to find my way out again. But my life had been guaranteed to last forever, and Lucifer wasn't like some of the other demons, to play tricks with his deals. If something happened, and I became trapped in Hell, Lucifer would either have to let me go or release the souls he took in exchange for my life.

Of course, I had promised Gabriel that I would never separate my soul from my body again. But then, I wasn't some angel, to put a centuries' old promise ahead of doing what was right.

CHAPTER 8

AFTER I RANG UP MY final customer and Madame Zarita and Dwayne had gone home for the evening, I turned the sign on the door to "Closed." The rickety stairs creaked as I walked up to the small apartment I kept on the floor above.

I pulled the string next to the bare light bulb that hung from the ceiling. Despite the differences in size and grandeur, my apartment in Philadelphia had much in common with my abode of three hundred years before, in Paris. To my left was a bookshelf with a number of dog-eared paperbacks and an assortment of rocks from when Bedlam went through his healing crystal phase. Next to that was a small pine desk that I didn't use so much for writing as I did for keeping the stuffed animals, scarves, and decorative boxes that Bedlam brought me from around the world. To my right sat my small bed with the crimson comforter that matched the curtains on the windows on the opposite wall.

I decided that I might as well make myself as comfortable as possible. Past experience had taught me that my body would behave as if it were dead, at least as far as motor control was concerned. Unfortunately, that meant that I was also susceptible to injury should I fall, and there was a large possibility that my muscles would cramp up if I left them in the same position for a long stretch of time.

I figured that I would be relatively safe if I lay on my bed for the duration of my absence. I stretched out and took a few deep breaths. The fact that I was actually going to journey to Hell was starting to sink in, and a shiver started at the base of my neck and spread to my fingers and toes.

I resolved to go before I imagined all the potential consequences of my actions.

It took me a few tries to get out of my body, but when I finally succeeded, the movement was as familiar to me as if no time had passed since I had last been in spirit form. I had to float downstairs to find a hellhole, but I located one in the middle of the diner's kitchen. The undulating fog was more ominous than I remembered, and had I a throat in this form, I would have gulped. It seemed impossible that something so clearly malicious could be invisible to the physical world. I wondered whether people were somehow aware of them and automatically avoided them, or a select few people could see them and thought they were hallucinating.

Enough stalling, I told myself. I had no body to brace, so I floated forward and lowered myself into the roiling smoke.

I felt a chill as I passed below the mist, and passed into a plane of impenetrable dark. I could neither see nor hear anything, and the air was as still as if I were buried in a cavern deep in the earth. I tried to scream but found I had no voice. I could not call Hell an empty void, though, because my unique sixth sense became overwhelmed with the pressure of innumerable souls suffering the desolation of Hell.

My first instinct was to retreat from the assault on every corner of my consciousness. I attempted to return the way I had come, but I did not know which way that was anymore, or even how to move through this blackness. But slowly I was able to perceive something, some kind of light or force that stood out from the hollowness that surrounded me. I could move toward this presence, and as I did so, I realized that there were other centers of activity.

I kept my momentum going toward the closest one.

As I grew nearer, I perceived shadows, seemingly cast from items outside my view, and heard the whisper of a breeze. I felt a draft on my legs and looked down in concern because, as far as I knew, I'd left my legs back on earth. Against the darkness, I could make out a shadowy foot that moved when I tried to take a step. I took a deep breath to calm myself but then realized that the fact that I was succeeding in doing so meant that I had lungs.

The souls whispered in my mind as I began to panic. I had always wondered what happened to people who went to Hell, and now I knew that they were doomed to spend eternity in this nothingness, with no hope of change or salvation.

Trapped here forever.

Lost in Hell.

No escape.

I took another deep breath, refusing to lose control. My body might have traveled with me to Hell, or it might have remained in my bedroom on earth. But regardless, I would never get any part of me back to earth if I stayed put. I took one hesitant step forward, and then another. I concentrated on keeping my breathing even as each stride made my spirit seem more substantial.

As my body solidified, so too did my environment. Walls coalesced around me, and I found myself walking down a dark hallway. I glanced behind me and found that the corridor stretched as far as the flickering candlelight allowed me to see. Shadows moved across the floor, though I couldn't see what monsters might have cast them. I reached a window, and a bolt of lightning revealed a forbidding landscape of bleak marshes and hardy vegetation akin to an English moor. If I tried, I could hear the wind howl across the plain and soft rumbles of thunder heralding a coming storm.

Through it all, the voices of the damned grew louder in

my mind. I could not distinguish individual human minds from the throng of the frenzied, endless cries, and if I had to endure only a few hours in their company, I would soon go as mad as any of them.

Join us, they seemed to whisper.

As I walked down the passageway, it seemed to shift before my eyes—first to the glyphed corridor at the temple of Isis where I met Bedlam, then to the walkway lined with brown stone pillars that led to the Oracle's seat at Delphi. For brief moments I felt the desert heat and then the wind against my back, but when I tried to focus on any one scene, I found myself back in the original hallway.

After a time, I passed through an entryway into a room lined on both sides with tall and sturdy wooden bookcases filled with leather-bound volumes. Closer inspection of the titles revealed them to be scholarly and religious works from every age and culture—Plato, Rousseau, Marx, Aristotle, the Egyptian *Book of the Dead*, the Vedas and the Upanishads, Sun Tzu, Confucius—all arranged in no particular order that I could discern. As I moved, the room shifted into other libraries that I had frequented over time, some filled with scrolls or tablets rather than books. But, again, if I concentrated, the room molded back into the austere library.

Nothing is real, murmured the souls.

In the center of the room, two worn brown leather armchairs sat on a burgundy-and-gold Persian rug facing a fireplace that gave off real heat. The fireplace bore painstakingly carved engravings inlaid with gold that must have been done by Hieronymus Bosch's evil twin. They depicted a hellscape of malformed bodies, writhing in agony amid inexorable flames. The images of those wretched souls matched only too well the bevy of damned souls still assailing my mind.

I heard only a slight whisper of fabric to warn me that I was not alone. I whirled around and beheld a tall, thin man considering me. I couldn't see him very clearly in the dim light, but I didn't need to. Only one person could belong to that backdrop, in the bowels of Hell. Closer inspection would reveal the greying black hair, slightly lined face, and impeccable dress of an aging professor, but that behind the delicate wire-rimmed glasses, his black eyes would swallow all the light in the room.

He is here.

"Hello, Mephistopheles."

After my expulsion from my village, I lived on my own for a time. I had never hunted before, but I learned, and soon I was able to trade with human villages for linens and copper tools. Often these villagers would offer me a place among them, but I worried I would bring my curse down upon them, so I kept my distance.

One evening, I had finished cooking my evening meal when a man approached me. I'd reached for my spear and kept a wary eye on him as he drew closer. I sensed from the power of his mind that he was no mere mortal, and his white linen robes appeared too pristine to have been made by human hands. His mind was equally clean-cut, ordered, and logical, with every thought fitting into a grander scheme solely of acquiring more knowledge.

"Greetings," this man said to me, and his outward geniality belied the cool calculation behind his eyes. He gestured to the fire. "May I join you?"

I nodded once and watched as he sat down opposite me, reaching out to warm his hands by the flames. He gazed at me as well, for a moment, gathering what information he could from my appearance. His black eyes paused on the scar left on my arm by Michael's flaming sword. I instinctively lifted my hand to cover it, and his mouth crooked up into a small smile.

I broke the silence first. "Who are you?"

"Such a simple question, yet one that begs the most complex of answers." He pulled his hands back from the fire and folded them together. "You may call me Mephistopheles."

"I'm Cama." I gave him the name I had been using since I left my village.

Silence stretched between us again. *I need only wait,* he thought. *She will speak when she cannot bear the silence anymore, and from that I will learn a great deal.*

I wanted to be contrary and wait for him to speak, but the hour grew late, and I did not wish him to remain once I had gone to sleep.

"You are like the man who came to our village." I hesitated to continue but decided that it would not hurt to simply ask a question. "Do you know...? Who was he? Why did he do that to us?"

I half expected him to not know what I was talking about, but I could tell that he not only did, but that he had come seeking information about that very incident.

"Knowledge is valuable. What would you trade me for such secrets as these?" He wanted to tell me everything, but he would say nothing if I couldn't give him something worthwhile.

"I have some food." I gestured to the fresh-cooked meat and barley cakes at my side, even while knowing such items, crucial to humans, were not the coin he traded in.

Mephistopheles laughed. "No material object could be as valuable as what is stored inside your head, my dear. I will make you a deal; I will tell you about your mystery man if you answer a few questions for me."

I agreed, but his disproportionate glee was almost enough to make me reconsider.

"We are angels, an older being than mankind, and more powerful." *And yet God expected us to serve them. Unthinkable!* "We are able to do things that they cannot, such as grant you immortal life."

"But... the other members of my village. He killed them and took them away."

He lifted his hands in a gesture of studied innocence. "You cannot expect something for nothing. The elders of your village knew that you had a power unlike any other. They thought that if you lived forever, so too would their village. So they offered the souls of any ten villagers in exchange for your immortal life."

I shook my head. "That doesn't make any sense. The elders hated my power."

Is there anything more amusing than the attempts of fools to compensate for their shortcomings? "Well, of course, as time went on, they regretted the deal they had made, and they feared that you would discover it. They thought if they pretended you had no power, or if no one else found out about it, they could get out of it."

I looked away from him, hoping he could not see the tears forming at the corner of my eyes. "Can you take it back? I don't want to live forever. I just want my family back."

I felt a flash of pity from him, but he stifled it before I could explore it further. "Only the one who made such a deal can reverse it, and I fear it would take the intervention of a higher power than you or me for Lucifer to relinquish those souls."

He gave me a minute to compose myself and then began grilling me about the details of my encounter with Lucifer. He was particularly interested in the details of how Lucifer had taken the souls. I described how Lucifer seemed to grab the souls out of the air and how the villagers fell dead. I didn't think I had much information to provide, but Mephistopheles seemed pleased with it.

A few centuries later, a man came to me, begging to get out of a contract he'd made for the cunning to unite several warring city-states. He had succeeded, and he feared the return of a man matching Mephistopheles's description. As more and more such cases came my way and the names of the demons began to change, I realized that Mephistopheles had used the information I provided to make his own demonic contracts and that he taught the other archdemons, as well, no doubt in exchange for some tidbit of knowledge they were loath to part with.

I was cagier in my interactions with Mephistopheles after that. He came to visit me every few centuries, always with a few pieces of intelligence that I would trade for. Though the feeling was not mutual, he seemed to rather like me. Nonetheless, if I had the misfortune to end up in the realm of any archdemon by accident, I was grateful that it was Mephistopheles's.

"Cama, what brings you here? Are you dead?" He shook his head, answering his own question. "No, of course not. If you were dead, you would not be coming to my domain."

Lost in Hell, hissed the souls of Hell.

I did not answer right away. I could barely process what he was saying, so onerous was the heaviness of the tortured souls on my mind. I could not feel Mephistopheles in my mind, so I could only assume that, despite my apparent solidity, my body was no more formed than those of the wailing spirits in the blackness.

"I see that my question does not have an easy answer." He gestured toward the leather chairs. "Well, come sit with me for a while. Perhaps we can come to a mutually beneficial agreement."

Stay with us.

I sank into the chair with relief, running my hands along the creases in the armrests. Taking the weight off my feet helped to ease some of the pressure on my mind, and I focused more of my attention on the astute presence before me.

"Tell me, Cama." He gestured to the room around us. "Tell me what you see here."

The question seemed innocent enough, but Mephistopheles did not ask innocent questions. "What will you give me in exchange?"

Nothing for free, whispered the souls of the damned.

He laughed. "Oh, my dear Cama, you have learned over the years. I will offer you this. If you tell me what you see, I will tell you why you see it."

Since I was curious as to how Hell had transformed before me from an incomprehensible nothingness into the seemingly solid room before me, and I also suspected that I would need more information from Mephistopheles before I left to find Azrael, I decided to play the game. "I see the library of a Gothic house."

He frowned. "Hell as a gothic mansion? I am disappointed. I expected something more original from you." He looked as if he expected me to defend myself, but I blinked, waiting for him to fulfill his end of the bargain. "Hell is largely unfathomable to the human mind, even one that has been around for centuries. We have found that humans tend to convince themselves that they are in an environment more familiar to them. A gothic mansion is a relatively common interpretation, and of course you would interpret my part of it as the library, the center of knowledge."

Know only pain.

I watched the room around me flicker to other "centers of learning" from my long life, only to return to the same gothic library.

It was still better than being in the black place.

Mephistopheles folded his hands and regarded me from over the top of them. "I find I have a number of questions for you at this point in time, my dear Cama. And I suspect that I have a great deal of information that would be of use to you, as well. Shall we trade, then? A question for a question?"

Play with us.

I so don't want to do this. "You disparage me for my lack of originality, yet you've been playing the same game since the beginning of time."

"Is that an acceptance?"

I nodded. I didn't see that I had much choice, and I did need to know how to get out of there and how to find Azrael. "By all means."

Mephistopheles folded his hands and pressed his peaked index fingers to his lips. "Well, first I must ask how you came to be here. In Hell, that is."

In Hell with us.

"I came through a hellhole."

He raised his eyebrows. "You can see hellholes? Fascinating. Even I cannot see one in my mortal form. Matter cannot pass through them, and you are not here in body, despite however you may appear to yourself."

"Wait, my body isn't really here?" I felt a wave of relief. "Why does it feel like it is?"

Mephistopheles sighed. "As I said, Hell is unfathomable to humans, and even your own form is subject to interpretation. You feel a body because you can better understand the world around you if you think you are experiencing it with your traditional senses." He paused. "Although I would be careful what damage you do to yourself here. If you believe your body to be hurt badly enough, no doubt it will also be damaged in the real world. And now it is my turn to ask a question, so I must wonder how you came to pass through a hellhole."

I bowed my head in acquiescence. "I can separate my spirit from my body. In that form, I can see hellholes and, apparently, pass through them."

You are nothing.

"Intriguing." He paused, likely to consider the ramifications of such a power. "An ordinary human would die, were his soul to be separated from his body. But you, of course, cannot die, so your body would remain free for you to return to it. No need to ask how you learned to do such a thing; this has Bedlam written all over it." He seemed satisfied with my answer to his question and motioned that it was my turn to ask.

I tried to prioritize all the things that I needed to know so that I gathered the most necessary information before he asked a question that I was unwilling to answer. "How do I leave here?"

Never to leave.

He tilted his head to the side. "Here as in Hell or here as in my realm?"

"Aren't they the same thing?"

"Yes—and then again, no. Leaving my domain will also let you out of Hell, but let us say that they are distinct enough that I choose to count them as different questions."

I sensed no deception from him, so I decided to accept this explanation, though I disliked that he was being contrary after reprimanding me for the same thing. "Very well, then how do I leave Hell?"

Never go home.

He nodded. "There are seven exits to Hell, one within the domain of each archdemon. These doors are hidden and may only be accessed with the permission of the demon himself. Now, usually the use of these doors is limited to demons, as the only humans who come here never depart. However, you are a special case, and Lucifer will almost certainly insist upon your release if he discovers that any of us holds you prisoner. Thus, should you become trapped in the realm of any archdemon, he—or she, I suppose—will likely offer you a method of release, though I cannot promise that the method of leaving will be easy or comfortable."

I suspected that he could, in fact, guarantee that whatever conditions the archdemons set for my being able to leave their territory would be both difficult and uncomfortable.

ELIZABETH CORRIGAN

"That will take me out of Hell, not back into black nothingness?"

Mephistopheles wrinkled his nose in disgust. "Why would I want a portal to the Abyss in my realm?"

I didn't understand why the archdemons wanted anything, but I didn't want to argue about it. At least I now knew that the Abyss Bedlam always complained about was the black nothingness. I gestured that Mephistopheles could ask his next question.

Nothing to understand.

"Tell me, Cama. Can you read my thoughts here, in this gothic Hell you have created for yourself?"

"No."

"Really?" From the malicious grin he gave me, I could only assume he was testing me by thinking something that would upset me to hear. But since I couldn't hear him, I decided to move on.

"When I go through a hellhole, how do I find Azrael?"

First mistake, the souls whispered.

His smile grew even wider, and I realized that I had given him the answer to what would have been his next question: What was I doing in Hell? No doubt he would have cursed himself for making such an amateur move in his favorite game. And while I wished I had asked a different question first, to prevent him from having the satisfaction of beating me, I was also grateful that the game would be over that much sooner.

His eyebrows furrowed. "You find her in the same way that you found me."

How much to tell him? "I wasn't trying to find you. I only detected that there were centers of activity, and I moved toward the closest one. They all appeared the same to me."

Always lost.

"Ah." Mephistopheles pursed his lips. "If you could not discern the identities of the powers here, I do not know how to teach you to do so. I can feel each of my fellow archdemons' presences, and each feels unique to me." He held up a hand as I opened my mouth to protest. "I recognize that this is not an answer to the question, so I will give you another piece of information for free, or at least save you from another question that I cannot answer. You will want to know how to get past Azrael to the door that she guards. I am unable to tell you that. I could hazard a guess as to the desires of my other fellows, but Azrael is the most... capricious of my compatriots. I can guarantee that she will require something far above and beyond what would be reasonable, but I cannot say what that might be."

He paused, doubtless waiting to see if I would protest the insufficiency of his answer; when I did not, he asked his next question. "So tell me, Cama, what makes you seek out Azrael?"

I did not want to tell him, not about Sebastian or his soul being sold, nor about how I had decided to save him. It would only lead to questions that I didn't want to answer, like why I felt the need to gainsay the system. He might also perceive it as a threat to the demonic way; after all, if I sought to rescue one of Azrael's souls, what was to stop me from doing the same to one of his. And, of course, I had to worry that he might warn Azrael that I was coming. But I still needed to ask him at least one more question if I wanted to get out, so I didn't have much choice.

Never a choice.

"She has laid claim to a soul that interests me." *Please don't let him ask any more specific questions. I don't want to get Sebastian away from Azrael only to make Mephistopheles find him interesting.*

Mephistopheles raised his eyebrows, probably as close to an admission of astonishment as I could get from him. "That is very..."—he paused, searching for the right word— "... *proactive* of you, Cama. I did not think that you were in the habit of interfering in the workings of Heaven and Hell. Might I ask what prompted this behavior?"

I gave him a small smile. "You may, after you answer my next question. You said you could hazard a guess as to what the other archdemons would require of me to leave their realms. So what will they ask?"

Only pain.

As I knew he would, he argued against my question. "Come now, Cama. You cannot seriously expect me to answer that as one question. Each archdemon is unique, and any information about escaping them would be a question on its own."

"I disagree," I replied. "First of all, you already answered two of the seven; you don't know what Azrael will ask, except that it will be unpleasant, and Lucifer feels honor-bound to release me based on the contract he made for my life and will thus require nothing from me. This leaves me with five remaining questions. However, four of those five will only be educated guesses on your part, since you cannot know for certain what any but yourself would require of me. I hardly think your hypotheses are worth a question each."

Worth nothing.

Mephistopheles stared at me for a moment with narrowed eyes. "My hypotheses, however, are based on the interpolation of large amounts of data that no one else has in their possession, and I cannot give such information away for free. I propose this: I ask you two more questions, for a total of three, and then I will tell you what you must do to get past each of the gates. That will equal one question for the way out of my domain and one question for each of the two others."

"Very well." For a demon, his fair offer was downright generous. "The answer to your first question is that I met a soul worth saving. What else do you want to know?"

He opened his mouth to protest my answer, but I gave

him what I hoped was a quelling look. He was already ahead in this game, and he knew it. "Well, I must know what made this soul so special. You have seen thousands of humans who have sold themselves to me and my fellows, and you have never made a movement to help them. In fact, you go out of your way to avoid them, and I believe you have told me that you find them particularly toxic. What is so special about this soul?"

Nothing special.

"Sold souls are so distasteful to me because they belong to people who belong in Hell. Even the ones who start off all right eventually collapse under the weight of knowing that they are damned. This one is different; he accepts an eternity in Hell as an acceptable cost for saving someone he loves, but it has not in any way damaged his character. He has acted only out of love and a desire to do good in the world. He does not belong in Hell, and if the rules do not—if God does not—allow for a way out of his contract, then I have to find it for him."

I had not meant to make such a speech, but I had been holding in my feeling on the subject for too long. I could not explain to Bedlam or Gabriel; Bedlam wouldn't understand the self-sacrifice, and Gabriel would try to stop me. And to have even my closest friends be unable to comprehend my actions would make me feel entirely alone in the world.

Mephistopheles studied me, and I wished that I could hear whatever he was thinking. But he was probably thinking something horrible, so I decided I was better off without it. "He sounds like a truly remarkable individual. How do you plan on wresting his soul from Azrael's clutches?"

Never let go.

"Is that your third question?" I asked. He indicated that it was, and I found that I had to laugh. "Honestly? I'm not sure. I'm hoping I can use my gift to determine what she wants more than his soul. With any luck, I can find something to trade her."

"You will forgive me if I doubt your ability to complete this task. In fact, I would go so far as to urge you to reconsider this course of action, which I can guarantee will end in sorrow. Even if you do manage to succeed, you are threatening a structure that has been in place for thousands of years. While you seem convinced of the virtue of your actions, I recommend that you also consider their wisdom."

He broke off and sat back in his chair. "Nevertheless, a bargain is a bargain, and I did promise to share information with you. Lilith will most likely come at you with her team of harpies; you will need to defeat not only her but also her followers. Beelzebub will want you to give him something that you value. Lethe will most likely want to use your gift to gain insight into her own situation, though listening to her scream will make you feel that you've paid five times the price of everyone else. And the Beast will only accept payment in blood."

Rip you apart.

I filed the information away, particularly as pertaining Lethe and the Beast, two of the archdemons with whom I had the least familiarity. "And what do you require?"

Mephistopheles's smile reminded me of a miser squeezing the last copper from a debtor. "The same thing I always require. The only coin I value is knowledge. In exchange for your release from my realm, I ask that you provide me with a piece of information that I do not have but that I would find more valuable than anything else you told me today. If you can think of nothing else, I will accept your true name."

Reveal yourself.

The old saying goes that names have power. I don't know if this is true for the average person, but it certainly is in my case. Not in the sense that faerie tales would have you believe; I did not have to do the bidding of whoever called me by my name. Nonetheless, there was a reason I changed my moniker throughout the ages, letting not even my companions know me by anything other than a pseudonym. Aside from me, only one being left alive in all of creation knew my name, and I had exerted considerable effort over the years to keep it so. Such a secret was, of course, extremely valuable to Mephistopheles. He had been trying to get it out of me for millennia, ever since he discovered that I had begun using different false names even before I met him.

Fortunately for me, I had recently received information that even the demon of intelligence would find even more desirable. "Earlier today, I spoke with the angel Keziel."

"Oh, really?" Mephistopheles asked, surprised. He must've truly thought he had found a way to trick my name out of me. "And what made the lovely angel of balance defy her celestial restraining order to seek you out?"

Can't break free.

"What did she say she wanted, or what did she actually want?"

Mephistopheles waved his hand dismissively. "What she said she wanted, of course. Her real reason was to see Bedlam; everyone knows that."

"She had a message for Gabriel." I reached back to what I had felt in her mind, trying to remember something that would be enough for Mephistopheles. "She wants him to return to his place in Heaven. I think something big is going to happen. It hasn't started yet, but the balance is going to change."

Closer to Hell.

Mephistopheles obviously wanted to tell me that my piece of information was insufficient for release from his realm, but we both knew it was enough.

He tapped his finger against the side of his mouth. "How interesting. That must mean..." He trailed off, no doubt seeking to tempt me with whatever this piece of intelligence meant to him.

I would not rise to the bait. "Are we done now?"

He gave an exaggerated sigh. "It seems you have kept your name from me yet again, Cama. But I'm sure there will be another time. I have, as always, enjoyed our conversation."

He snapped his fingers, and I let out a sigh of relief that I could finally escape the screaming souls pounding on my mind. The fire disappeared in a puff of smoke, and the mouth of the fireplace widened and lengthened. The images of the damned elongated, stretching along the span of the opening until they formed an ornate frame to the doorway that now stood in front of us. Through it, I saw only a black deeper than a moonless night.

You'll be back.

I took a deep breath and stepped through.

CHAPTER 9

I COULDN'T SEE. *Am I home?* The question seemed important, but I couldn't focus, couldn't even remember what home was. Then things became clearer, and I realized that there was a light past the darkness.

I opened my eyes. I lay in my bed, right where I had been before I sent myself to Hell. *Holy crap, I actually did it. I went to Hell.* I took a deep breath. *But now I'm back.*

I heard the mind of someone next to me. *But if I wanted that many chickens, I would have gone to a different deli... Ooh, she's waking up.*

"Where did you go, Khet?" Bedlam asked me. I tried to determine if he guessed the truth, but I couldn't get a clear read from him.

I rolled up onto my side and looked at him. He was maintaining a perfect poker face, which I supposed was easy to do when no single emotion controlled his mind for more than a microsecond. *Bright side?* I thought. *At least he doesn't know that Keziel was here.* If he knew that, there would be exactly one thought on his mind.

"Nowhere. I've been right here all evening." I glanced at the clock to check the time. "Wait. It is still this evening, right? I saw you this morning?"

"Khet, if you wanted me to believe that you hadn't gone anywhere, that argument was not the most effective means of convincing me." He stepped over to my bed, and I moved to give him room to sit next to me. He stretched out his legs next to mine and wrapped his arm around my shoulder.

I leaned my head against his chest, and he laid his head on top of mine.

"Promise you won't get mad?"

He laughed and pulled me closer for a moment. "Khet, with all the stupid crap that I've pulled over the ages, it would be beyond hypocritical of me to get mad at you."

We were silent for a bit as I tried to think of a way to explain.

"This is about that Sebastian kid, isn't it?"

"It's just... he doesn't belong in Hell. It's not fair." I sounded a bit whiny, even to my own ears. "And I know that the world isn't fair. More than anyone, I know that. But I think that maybe it never will be if we stand by and let things like this pass. God made us, and He won't stand up for us when we need Him to. And I can't fix all the problems, even all the problems that I cause. But maybe I can fix this."

"I understand." I must have looked skeptical because he insisted, "I do, really. No one rails against things that everyone else deems unchangeable more than I do. But I would like to know where you went, so that if you don't come back, I know where to find you."

"The only way I could think to help Sebastian was to find Azrael. And the only way I could think to find Azrael was..."

"To go to Hell?" *Wow, like that isn't the worst idea ever.* "Did you find her?"

"Not yet. But I ran into Mephistopheles, and he was in a helpful mood."

Bedlam held his arm more tightly around me for a moment. *I trust her, but really. Worst. Idea. Ever.* "Khet, are you sure that you know what you're doing?"

"I am almost certain that I don't. But I can't continue to do nothing." I realized that I meant that about more than the situation with Sebastian—I meant it about my entire life. I had spent millennium after millennium standing on the sidelines, doing nothing with my powers for fear of making the world a worse place or fear of losing my own comfort. I needed to know that I believed in something, that I stood for anything other than being some kind of cosmic doormat. And maybe I needed to risk losing everything in order to discover what I had.

"Well, be careful." He kissed the top of my head. "There are some of us who would miss you if anything happened to you." He paused for a moment and then started giggling, as he pictured what would happen if I told Gabriel about my trips to Hell. I gave him a stern look, and he sobered. "Yeah, don't tell Gabs. He won't take it well."

That was an understatement. I sank down deeper into my plush pillows. "Well, apparently taking a trip to Hell can be tiring, so I am going to sleep. You can stay if you want—or not, as you choose."

He elected to stay, and I fell asleep with the cacophony of Bedlam's mind keeping me safe from the rest of the world.

Bedlam was no longer next to me when I woke up the next morning, and utensils clattered in the kitchen downstairs. I glanced at the clock and noticed that it was an hour after I was supposed to open. *I'm sure Dwayne can handle things for a little while.* I started to close my eyes again to grab a few minutes more sleep when I remembered that it was Dwayne's day off. Which meant Bedlam was probably in the kitchen, and leaving him alone in there was about as wise as letting a fox who really liked to paint things blue into your pristine white henhouse. I showered and dressed, then went downstairs.

There was an elderly couple sitting at one of the tables. Since they were drinking coffee instead of drumming their fingers on the menus, I assumed that someone had waited on them. Since they weren't spitting the coffee across the table and cursing the ancestry of whoever poured it, I knew it wasn't Bedlam. Which was probably an even better thing than usual, because the chaos demon huddled over the jukebox, barely keeping a lid on his seething rage.

A familiar presence moved around in the kitchen, one I trusted far more than I did Bedlam—at least as far as food was concerned. "Gabriel's in the kitchen?"

"Yeah, he's making breakfast," Bedlam responded as he jabbed a button on the jukebox. Today was apparently not a dancing day, as the room was filled with the first few power chords of Bon Jovi's "You Give Love a Bad Name."

If I hadn't already known that only one thing could make Bedlam as angry as he was, the song would have cued me in to what was going on with him. "Do you want to talk about it?"

"Talk about what?" He didn't turn around to look at me. "My unsettling impulse to play loud '80s music, first thing in the morning?"

"No." I took a step closer to him. "Do you want to talk about Keziel coming to visit me yesterday?"

"Not really." I waited because I knew he didn't mean it. "What did she want, anyway?"

"The usual. She had an allegedly urgent message for Gabriel, but she really wanted to remind me that it's her choice and not mine that she stays away." *But mostly she came to see you*, I thought, but I didn't say it, because she didn't want me to know that was the reason she came, and because it would only hurt Bedlam more.

"You weren't going to tell me she was here, were you?" Even though he didn't want to see her, even though he understood why I didn't tell him, he was angry with me. I tried not to take it personally, because he was actually angry with Keziel—for choosing Jophiel over him, for not letting him alone, for ruining his life. And more than that, he was angry with himself—for letting her affect him so much, for not preventing Jophiel from taking her in the first place, for not being the kind of ex-celestial being that

106

she would give up everything for.

"No." I didn't know what to say. I never knew what to say to Bedlam when he got like this. "I'm sorry. I didn't want to hurt you, and I was hoping you wouldn't know she had been here."

He whirled around and glared at me. "Of course I knew she was here! How many times do I have to explain it to you? Whenever anything even hinting of chaos happens, I know it. And that's for little things, like a clock decreasing in accuracy. When the fourth most powerful angel in creation openly defies the second most powerful one, she might as well cut the words 'Keziel was here' into the fabric of the universe!"

"I'm sorry." *Useless. I am so totally useless.*

"Sorry?" He advanced on me. "What are you sorry for? Sorry that you couldn't prevent me from getting angry? Because you're the almighty, all-powerful Khet, and you have to control how everyone feels?"

I knew I shouldn't try to reason with him, and I should just let his rage burn out, but I couldn't bear to watch him in this kind of pain. "No, Bedlam. I hate to see you hurt this badly."

His eyes flashed. "The fact that you think for one second that you can spare me this pain by keeping one secret shows that you have no idea what you're talking about. You think you're special because you get to live forever, because you can see some of what goes on inside our heads, but you're still a human. You cannot even begin to fathom what it's like to know that the only person you will ever love will never be with you. It never goes away and only ever subsides a small amount, until, inevitably, something happens to make it flare back up. And it will always flare back up. A voice, a color, a smell, any little thing can suddenly remind you, and it's like it happened yesterday." And in his head I saw and felt all the things that reminded him of Keziel: the deep timbre of her voice, the shade of green she wore, the scent of hyacinth—and, combined with all these things, the intensity with which he loved her.

"Bedlam..."

"Stop! Just stop!" He picked up a glass and threw it across the room toward the empty tables. It hit the wall and shattered. "You can't fix everything, Khet! And you especially can't fix me!" Then he disappeared.

I felt tears form at the corners of my eyes, but I took a deep breath and resolved not to think of it anymore. Bedlam was upset, and he didn't mean what he said, and in a few days he'd be back, begging for my forgiveness.

I turned to the elderly couple, who stared open-mouthed at the place where Bedlam stood. "I'm so sorry about that. He's a student at the University of the Arts, and sometimes he gets carried away with his rehearsals."

The woman turned her head to look at me. "Did he... did he vanish into thin air?"

I let out a little laugh. "No, of course not. That's impossible."

She nodded, but she wasn't sure she believed me.

I went back to the kitchen, where Gabriel was flipping fried eggs onto plates already piled with sausage links, bacon, and toast. "That the food for the occupied table?"

He nodded. "Is Bedlam okay?"

I reached over and picked up the plates. "Is Bedlam ever okay after a Keziel visit?" He opened his mouth to say something, but I shook my head and walked out the door.

The jukebox had cycled onto its next song—"Don't You Want Me" by The Human League—and it looked as though I was in for a line of bitter breakup songs until Bedlam returned to reset it. I shook my head and carried the food over to the elderly couple.

She mixed up our orders, the woman thought as I started to turn away. *Where did that nice-looking waiter go?*

"I'm so sorry." Before they had time to do it, I reached

down and switched their plates.

The woman narrowed her eyes at me. *How did she know that?*

I mentally kicked myself. "Would you like some more coffee?" I didn't wait for an answer before walking over to the counter and grabbing the coffee pot. I refilled their mugs then almost banged into Madame Zarita walking through the door. I managed to avoid spilling coffee on her, but it was a near thing.

She peered at me. "Are you all right, dearie?"

I gave her what I hoped was a reassuring smile. "I'm fine. It's been a bit of a hectic morning."

She nodded. "Well, remind me later, and I'll show you some new pictures of little Anthony. You won't believe how big he's getting."

I promised I would look at the pictures of her grandchildren when I got a break, and she made her way to her booth in the back. I swept up the bits of the glass that Bedlam had destroyed and wiped the area with a wet paper towel. About the same time that I decided my floor should be safe enough for any unsuspecting shoeless passerby, Gabriel emerged from the kitchen, carrying a plate of waffles.

I smiled at him as I threw away the paper towel. "You made my favorite."

"Theoretically, yes." He looked askance at the plate. "But I think that Bedlam might have done something to the batter before you came down."

"Let's try them. It can't possibly be worse than the time he put the entire box of baking soda into the cookie dough." Gabriel conceded that this was true and handed me a plate. I pulled some silverware, butter, and syrup from their respective residences behind the counter, then prepared my waffles and took a bite. I was pleasantly surprised to find the waffles were flavored with butterscotch, but then I quickly perceived a second, much less compatible taste.

"Are these jalapeños? How did he manage to cut up

jalapeños and get them in the batter without me noticing?" Gabriel was so befuddled that I laughed. After a moment, he saw the humor in the situation and allowed himself a smile.

Later, after we had made and eaten another batch of waffles, and rang up the elderly couple, Gabriel announced that he was spending the day with me. Having Gabriel around was in many ways better than having Bedlam, not the least of which was that he actually helped out. He insisted on doing all the cooking for me. By some strange coincidence, Gabriel was a better cook than I was, and the few customers I had sent their compliments back.

Maybe I should have him stick around. The diner's reputation would be back up in a heartbeat. I chuckled at my own thought. I wanted Gabriel to stay, all right, but that wasn't anywhere near the top reason.

"What's so funny?" Gabriel walked out of the kitchen and started around the counter.

"Oh. You know." I gestured to the small pile of dishes that was forming by the sink. "Plates."

He pulled out a stool and sat down. "Plates are funny?"

"They can be." *Wow, Carrie. That is the lamest thing you have ever said. Change the topic. Change the topic now.* "So what have you been up to for the last few months?"

"Since I last saw you? Let me think." Gabriel tapped his fingers to the beat of the latest song on the jukebox (Matchbox Twenty, "Disease"). "Well, first I went to Atlanta to work on a Habitat for Humanity project..."

As he talked, I found myself staring at his fingers as they drummed the table. They were perfect, like the rest of him, and long and thin, like they were designed for playing a musical instrument. And though he spent all his time doing hard labor, he recreated them anew every time he appeared, so they were soft as silk. I found myself wondering what it would be like to feel those fingers laced with mine. Gabriel had touched me before, of course, but always for just a few seconds, always followed by an apology for invading my space. He didn't realize that feeling his skin brush against mine electrified me in a way that nothing else did.

"Cassia?" He lifted those fingers to wave in front of my face. I must have zoned out while he was talking. I realized I had my elbows on the counter and was leaning on my hands.

"Sorry." I lifted my eyes to his and made a small attempt at a smile.

"You were a million miles away." For a moment, he seemed sad that he couldn't hold my attention, but that was my own wishful thinking. Sometimes it seemed like my powers always failed when I needed them the most. And with Gabriel, I got so lost in his light that I imagined things that weren't there.

I straightened up and wiped the crumbs from the counter off my arms. "Contemplating where to go on my next vacation. Bedlam and I were thinking Greece. We haven't been there in centuries."

"You could come with me, if you wanted. I'm going to Ghana to distribute AIDS medication." His eyes lit up as they said it, but I suspect that had more to do with his trip than the anticipation of my presence. "You could do so much good for these people just by talking to them. You always know what to say, and these people often feel that they have no one to understand their pain."

"I do not always know what to say. Sometimes I feel like I never do." *Take Bedlam, for one.* But I didn't want to talk to Gabriel about Bedlam.

"You really care about everyone, and that's exactly what these people need."

"I wish I could, Gabriel." And on some level I did. I wished that I could be with Gabriel always, and I wished that I could help these people who so desperately needed it. "But you know that I can't. When I'm around all those people who are suffering, I get so overwhelmed by all the negative emotions, and I can't help anyone."

It made me feel guilty, that I could not get past my own limitations in order to help people who needed it and that I really was far more comfortable in the security of my diner than I was in destinations destroyed by disease, war, and poverty. And if I were being totally honest, part of my reason for saying no was that I had already lived thousands of years without things like running water and air conditioning, and I had no desire to repeat those experiences. Gabriel frowned at my response, and I couldn't help but feel that he was disappointed in me, for not being able to put my own needs aside in order to help other people.

"I forgot to tell you," I said, changing the subject. "Keziel had a message for you."

"She did?" He had been the recipient of many such "messages" before and knew as well as everyone else that they were rarely as urgent as she portrayed them.

"Well, she said she did. But she wouldn't leave it with me." I paused, considering. "Whatever it was, it did have her worried. I think she wants to ask you to go back again. To Heaven, I mean."

Gabriel saddened, as he did whenever he thought about what he left behind in Heaven. "Maybe she's right. Maybe I should go back. I've been away for so long, and I have seen nothing to make me think that my place in the universe should change. Maybe it's time I admit defeat and go back to doing what I am supposed to."

"You know I can't tell you what to do." I hoped he could not detect that my heart sped up and my breath became a little shallower every time he said that he might return to Heaven. He visited me now, but if he returned to his position as archangel, I would run into him every few centuries at most. More likely Michael would keep him so busy that I would never see him at all. "But you left for a reason, and if you don't figure out what that reason is and come to terms with it, you are going to be in the same position you were in when you left."

He gave me a small smile. "You're right, of course. But sometimes I think that what I want is not nearly so important as what the world needs. And maybe Keziel and Michael are right, and they really need me back, where I can do some real good, not just the little things I do now."

"First of all, what you do are not little things. I could not possibly count the number of lives you've saved—and anyway, you know as well as I do that the value of a single life cannot be measured on some kind of numeric scale. Second, I think you said that Keziel might be right about something, and you know that's absurd."

He smiled at me again. He didn't dislike the female angel as much as I did—he didn't dislike anyone—but even he knew there was some truth in what I was saying. "Well, it's getting late, and I have a few things that I want to do before I go to the clinic tomorrow. I'll probably stop by when I'm done there."

"I'll be here."

As always, I was disappointed to see him go, but now that he was gone—and wouldn't be back for almost twenty-four hours—it meant I could make another trip to Hell that night, without interference.

CHAPTER 10

I THOUGHT THAT KNOWING WHAT WAS coming for me would make the second trip to Hell easier. I recalled the crushing of all the lost souls and tried to brace myself for a repeat of the inundation. But when I passed through the hellhole the second time, I realized that my memory had been unable to recall the true horror of every tortured soul since the beginning of time forcing the suffering of its existence onto my fragile psyche.

Welcome back to Hell, they whispered.

Some things were easier, though. It did not take me nearly as long to identify the different centers of gravity now that I knew they were the archdemons. I spent some time trying to distinguish them from one another so that, should I need to make multiple trips, at least I would not mistakenly visit the same archdemon twice. Once I had identified the seven different forces, I tried to see if I sensed any differences about them that might help me tell which one was Azrael. But even knowing which was Mephistopheles did not enable me to discern any unique characteristics of each of the locations. I decided I had no choice but to go to each one in turn and hope that Azrael's came sooner rather than later.

I selected a locus and moved toward it. As before, my body and surroundings slowly solidified until I walked down a corridor similar to the one I had used to reach Mephistopheles. As I moved, my surroundings shifted into other locations, an empty thoroughfare in Rome or the alley behind my diner, but they always settled back into the original candle- and lightning-lit hallway when I tried to focus on any detail.

After a time, I came to a doorway, and when I stepped through, I found myself in the dining room of the gothic mansion. I thought the arrangement of baguettes reminiscent of the customary display at the bakery I worked at in Paris, and the fruits were laid out in the same manner that Gnaeus spread them out for a banquet. I glanced up at the fluorescent lights, thinking they too seemed out of time, but then they were gone, replaced by a chandelier with more than two dozen candles held aloft by ropes of twisted gold. I made out a set of carvings on the mahogany furniture that looked to match the fireplace in Mephistopheles's library, with faces that seemed to writhe in the flickering light. They even appeared to take on the voices of the tortured souls.

Free us.

The long table was set with fine china and silverware and covered with serving platters bearing the most tantalizing meats imaginable: a turkey stuffed with sage- and marjoram-seasoned breadcrumbs, a roast cooked to pink perfection, and a whole pig complete with a ruby red apple in its mouth. The meats were surrounded by platters overflowing with grapes, peaches, plums, and assorted other juicy fruits, as well as bowls overflowing with potatoes, turnips, and corn. Lining the maroon walls of the room were any number of sideboards brimming with buttery crusted rolls and cakes drizzled with chocolate syrup.

I did not need to see the rotund man sitting at the head of the table to know that I had entered the realm of the archdemon Beelzebub.

I had met Beelzebub only once before, and neither of us had made a positive impression on the other. I was living in a cave near Delphi in Greece, aiding those who came to see me. My name at the time was Corinna, but I was more commonly known in the surrounding regions as the Oracle. History has often confused me with the Pythia of Apollo's temple, but that was intentional on my part. I had learned the benefits of having a cover "Oracle" who sent me cases that were beyond her abilities.

Weeks could pass between visitors. After living in a crowded area of Egypt, I enjoyed spending the time in solitude. The activities of maintaining a home in a cave took most of my time. I had to keep the fire built at all times if I wanted to eat and not freeze to death. Sometimes I went down to civilization for food, and other times I relied on the hunting skills that I had taught myself the first time I tried to live alone. And on days where my clothes were clean and I had plenty of dry firewood, I sat on the side of the mountain and got lost in thought while I enjoyed the feel of the sun on my skin.

One day, I felt the presence of two angels outside my cave, and as I drew closer, they raised their voices in some kind of argument. One I recognized as Bedlam, who had sought me out in Egypt a few years previously, and the other was a being that I had not previously encountered, though I immediately recognized him as a demon because of his strong and malevolent presence.

I walked to the mouth of the cave and saw Bedlam in conflict with a tall, corpulent man with curly red hair. Given the dark nature of his thoughts, I was surprised to find that his mind, on the surface, appeared like a buoyant light that could not help but shine upon those who came into contact with it. But as I looked closer, I realized that beneath the surface, the demon's spirit had rotted to the core, so that where it had once spread generosity, it now engendered gluttony in all it encountered.

"... leaving, and you can't make me stay," Bedlam was saying as I approached the pair.

The portly man reached out and put a hand on Bedlam's shoulder. "Be reasonable. I know you're not necessarily happy with the way things are, but we cannot change that. All of us would like to return to Heaven, but we cannot do that by going off on our own. We must retain some sense of order and decorum."

"You think this is about getting back into Heaven?" Bedlam yanked his arm out of the other demon's grasp. "I don't give an angel's eyelash about Heaven. Things were just as aggravating back then, with everyone telling me what to do."

I would ask Bedlam about this later, and he would tell me that the one thing that almost all angels and demons had in common was an overwhelming need to maintain their hierarchy. Each angel knew exactly where he or she was in relation to every other angel above and below him or her, and every angel accepted the right of those above him or her to give orders and expect them to be obeyed. The Fall had, of course, distorted this to some degree, but Lucifer quickly set up a hierarchy with all the demons having a boss to whom they could report, and Michael had taken control of the forces of Heaven and reinforced the hierarchy, gaps and all. Bedlam was the one exception to this, and the smallest thing he did could have the order-obsessed angels in hysterics.

"You know that we give you a lot of leeway." Beelzebub crossed his arms and gave Bedlam a stern look. "If you don't want to work with Lethe anymore, maybe we can find something else for you to do. I don't think that Mephistopheles has had the pleasure of your company for a few centuries now..."

"Seriously, Belsy, why do I have to work with anyone?" Bedlam bounced up and down on his feet like a petulant child. "Not one of you likes me even a little bit. Wouldn't you all be happier if I went my own way?"

"Because there are only two sides in this war, Bedlam, and you picked yours."

117

"The war is over. It's been over forever. We lost. What you're fighting is not the continuation of a war. It's a pathetic attempt to... to... I don't even know what you're trying to achieve! Why do we have to be achieving anything anyway?"

Beelzebub glanced in my direction and noticed that I was standing there. "It seems we have company, Bedlam. Is this the... person... you were looking for?"

"Khet!" Bedlam bounded over to me. "Tell Belsy I don't have to do his evil bidding if I don't want to!"

"I apologize for the interruption." The other demon approached me at a much more sedate pace. He gave me a smile, the kind of smile you see on a goat merchant who is about to offer you an unbeatable deal that will result in you owning five goats about to be bleating at death's door. "My name is Beelzebub, and I'm afraid that my operative has been harassing you unduly. I assure you that this is not the kind of behavior that we ordinarily sanction, and I wanted to come here myself and assure you of that."

I smiled back at him. "My name is Corinna, and it's really not a problem. Part of being who and what I am is that people from all walks of life come to me from a variety of locations. I learned to accept that long ago."

"Well, that's good to know." Beelzebub smiled at me, but his eyes remained hard and cold. "Now, the problem we are having here is that Bedlam seems to think that your advice regarding his future holds some weight, and I would appreciate it if you would tell him that it's really for the best if he return to Hell with me."

I looked past Bedlam's smiling façade to the emotions underneath. *Oh, please don't tell me to go back to Hell. They'll send me back to the Abyss. Dark. Cold. Endless. I'm not doing that again.*

Beelzebub, on the other hand, was quite gleeful at the prospect of having Bedlam in his grasp. *Oh, come on already and tell him to go away, girl. He's in for it, this time. Lucifer's letting me send him so far out he'll never make it back.*

"That's strange, that you would say that." I doubt my smile was any more sincere than his. "Because he seems to think that it would not be to his benefit at all."

"Oh, nonsense!" Beelzebub gave a jolly laugh. "I don't know what kind of stories he's been telling you, but I assure you..."

"He has told me nothing," I allowed my voice to go cold. "If you know who I am, you should know better than to try to fool me. I know what you intend, and I know that you cannot force him to go. If you want someone to endorse your torture methodology, you will have to go elsewhere. I am not in the habit of telling people what to do. However, you did come to ask me for a boon, so I will give you one, though not the one you sought. I will tell you what I see when I look at you. You, like most of your demon kin, claim that you seek a return to your favored positions in Heaven, but you know that this is not true. You know what you would need to do to return to God's grace; you have always known. Yet instead you continue to fight a war that you lost long ago, using the same tactics that have been unsuccessful time and time again. You cling to the notion that you cannot change, and you continue to dig yourselves deeper into the hole of your own self-pity. And the reason you hate Bedlam so much is not that he does not listen to you but that he questions you. And if you want someone to tell you what to do, then this is what I say: Return to Hell, and never seek a seat around my fire again."

"Why, you..." The jolly merchant demeanor vanished to be replaced by that of a red-faced drunk, prepared to harm anyone who stood in his way. He lifted a giant fist to strike me.

Bedlam teleported in front of me in time to block him. "Careful, Belsy! You know she's one of Luci's deals, and he won't like it if you touch her!"

Beelzebub growled and menacingly shook his fist at me. "This isn't over!"

I would have laughed in his face at his clichéd empty threat, but I decided that would worsen the situation. I let him dematerialize in peace.

Bedlam turned around and looked at me, his brow furrowed with concern. "That might not have been the smartest thing you've ever done. Belsy only *looks* cheerful. In reality, he has a vicious temper and a long memory." Then he brightened and looked at me expectantly. I felt as though I had acquired a new puppy, one with the capacity to make the entire planet stop spinning on its axis. "So... What do you have to do around here? Ooh, I know! There's a great farm at the bottom of this mountain. Have you ever tipped a cow?"

"Well, well, well. If it isn't little Corinna, come to see me in my home," the red-haired demon greeted me. He seemed to have prepared for my arrival, so I assumed that Mephistopheles had been telling tales of my quest. He waved a hand bearing a large turkey leg at the seat next to him. "Please, please, sit! Enjoy the feast."

Stay forever.

I sat in the chair he indicated, placing the napkin to my left in my lap without thinking. He flourished his haunch of meat over my plate, and the dribbles of grease that fell morphed into my favorite foods: flaky buttermilk biscuits, spinach and mushrooms sautéed in garlic, and roasted lamb with a cherry glaze. The goblet on my right filled with something that appeared to be red wine, though given the company, I would not have been surprised to find that it was the blood of a virgin or something equally disturbing. Under normal circumstances, my mouth would have watered, but the wailing of thousands of dead souls echoing in my head interfered with my appetite. That, combined with the fact that so many mythologies had tales about the perils of consuming anything in the underworld, made me more than a little hesitant to sample any of the bounties before me.

"Now, Corinna, it has been too long since we've seen each other. You simply must tell me what you've been up to." As ever, the demon had a jovial expression that served as a skin for his snake-like interior. I could not read his thoughts, but I could see the cold glint in his eye.

One of us.

Based on his geniality, I assumed Beelzebub had decided to play a sort of game with me. He would not break the pretense that I was a welcome guest as long as I did not. Like Mephistopheles's question game, the ploy lacked originality, but most angels from either side had never been especially concerned about their own triteness. They claimed they were the ones who had made the clichés in the first place.

"Oh, you know." I struggled to focus on my words and not the cacophony of souls outside. "I've been doing... things. Mostly working in bars, but a few decades back, I purchased a diner, and I spend most of my time there."

Not special.

"A diner?" He laughed in the manner reminiscent of Santa Claus, which was not surprising, given that the Santa myth had many of its roots in the actions of the demon of generosity. I doubt that the Christian groups who note how much Santa and Satan have in common realize how close they are to the truth. Of course, the saccharine Santa who brings presents to good children bears far less resemblance to the original than the pagan myths involving the slaughter of bad children.

"Tell me, how does that work for you, staying in the same place for decades? Don't people notice that you never age?"

I raised my glass to my lips and pretended to take a sip.

The scent confirmed that it contained a red wine. That was a mistake on his part; I preferred white. "I can go for longer than you think without people getting too suspicious, but after ten years or so, it's hard to convince people that I'm pushing thirty. So I go on an extended vacation for a few months, then pretend to be a niece coming in to take care of the place. Surprisingly few people bother to question it."

No interest.

His thick fingers tore the slick skin off the meat in his hand. "I find it so fascinating that someone of your years and abilities remains so in the shadows. In this day and age, you could make a fortune with some good publicity; and with a solid investment plan, even you would not need to worry about your future. I could definitely connect you with some of the right people, if you wanted to go in that direction."

I bet you could. "I'll have to keep that in mind." I picked up my fork began to toy with the spinach, separating it from the mushrooms, keeping as much attention as I could on something more solid than the unpleasant emotions that surrounded me. "And how has business been going for you?"

"Oh, you know, I can't complain." He took a large bite of meat off his bone and continued to speak while chewing. "Though I must say that the quality of human souls seems to be ever-diminishing. No one comes up with any good wishes. It's always 'a million dollars.' Like that's even enough to live on anymore."

Poor in spirit.

"The times do change." He was trying to bait me with distasteful words, but if he thought that he could get me to lose my temper as easily as I had that day back in Delphi, he was mistaken. For one thing, I did not have Bedlam to protect here; and for another, I was not stupid enough to anger him in his own domain, where he could rearrange matter at whim. Besides, my throbbing head could not condone the yelling.

"So, Corinna, I find that after all these years, I rather owe you a debt of gratitude."

I was surprised to find that there was some sincerity in his words, though I could not imagine what he would thank me for. "Indeed?" I took another fake sip of wine.

"Yes." He reached around the roast in front of him to grab a fistful of grapes. "Well, really, all of us archdemons do. You see, you managed to take away any of our responsibility for Bedlam's absurd behavior, so none of us have to waste our time trying to forestall his ill-advised behavior. Really, all of us are quite impressed at your ability to tolerate him."

False words.

Ah, so the new plan was to insult my friend and attempt to make me feel responsible for the chaos he caused. While my first impulse was to come to Bedlam's defense, since most of the things he did were only upsetting if you were an order-obsessed angel, I decided to be satisfied with Beelzebub's jealousy that I had managed to keep Bedlam's loyalty for longer than anyone else.

"You are, of course, welcome for any assistance I have provided on that score." I took a beat to try to clear my head before broaching the next subject. "And, as it turns out, I think I have a way that you can repay your 'debt,' as you term it."

"Really?" He brought the grapes to his mouth and ate nearly the entire bunch in one massive bite, though a single piece of fruit detached and rolled onto his plate.

No chance.

"Yes. You see, I arrived at your banquet entirely by chance, and I would appreciate it if, after we finish our conversation, you would be so kind as to grant me passage out of Hell."

"Hmm..." Beelzebub tapped his finger on his lips and made a great show of considering my request, though he had no intention of letting me go that easily. Even if he

were not interested in retaliation for my behavior the first
time we met, it would be unthinkable for a demon to give
something away and get nothing in return. "Well, Corinna,
I would like to be able to extend such a favor to you, but
it is not easy for me to create a door such as you ask. The
energy cost of creating a portal that can bridge dimensions
in this manner is great, and I would not want to undertake
it without ensuring that it was truly of value to you. Yes,
I believe I would need a token to show your dedication to
returning to earth."

Give up everything.

I nodded as if I believed that allowing me to pass through
the door would be any more difficult for him than blinking
an eye. "And what type of token would you require as a
testament of my earnestness?"

"It would have to be something of great value to you."
He speared the wayward grape with his fork, causing little
spurts of juice to spray over his greasy plate. "And it must
be something that you would carry with you into Hell. I
think that an appropriate price would be a memory."

"A memory?" I was more surprised by his cost than I
should have been. I suppose I had expected him to request
something to be paid upon my return to earth or something
that a fiend could go and claim for him. "I was not aware
that you could collect memories. I always thought that
was under the domain of..."

"My colleague Lethe? Ordinarily, you would be correct.
However, several centuries back, I realized the value of
being able to exact payment in the non-corporeal realms,
and she devised a method by which I can remove memories
from souls in my domain." He reached into his pocket and
pulled out a glass ball. "It's very simple. You tell me that
you are willing to pay the price, and I will extract the
memory from your brain. It will be as if it never happened
for you."

Nothing left.

I felt a flash of gratitude that the price he asked was so small, and I immediately regretted it. I had any number of memories that I would not mind losing, but certainly those would not be the ones that Beelzebub would focus on. I had already begun to catalog the memories that were most important to me before I realized that this was exactly what he expected me to do. He looked into the glass sphere and seemed able to view my memories through it as I experienced them.

"Let me see." He could barely restrain his glee at my falling so easily into his trap. "I think this one will do." He shook the ball and stopped my thoughts to focus on a single scene, as if my mind were some kind of Rolodex that he could control. I gazed into the sphere and realized that it showed a reflection of the event occurring in my brain, stealing my thoughts like some demonic snow globe.

Steal your soul.

A tiny version of myself hummed as I prepared dinner while my husband Hamin sat at a table fiddling with a hand scythe. He was always trying something new with his tools, convinced that if he found the right wood for the handle or the right angle of the blade he could speed up harvesting time by a significant margin. I wasn't really paying attention to his thoughts, but one stood out to me: *I have to remember to thank Amie for offering to give us the crib Vara's getting too big for, but it doesn't look like we'll be needing it this year.*

"I wouldn't be too sure of that." As soon as I spoke, I regretted it. Hamin didn't mind when I used my powers, but if the Elders got wind of it, they wouldn't be happy.

Hamin looked up from his tool. "What are you saying?"

My cheeks flushed. "I... nothing."

He stood up and walked over to me. "Are we going to have a baby?"

I couldn't bring myself to look at him. "Maybe."

He knew me well enough to take that as an affirmation. "That's wonderful news! Why didn't you tell me?"

"I just... It's so hard to be certain, and I wanted to be sure this time before I told you, because you were so disappointed when the last one was a false alarm." I looked up and gave him a small smile. "But I am pretty sure now. By the fall harvest we should have a need for the cradle, after all."

Hamin beamed, and I don't think I had ever seen him so happy. I returned his expression with equal enthusiasm. He leaned down to kiss me, and I felt like we had to be the happiest couple in the world.

The orb froze on the embracing couple, and the emotional currents I associated with it ground to a halt inside my head. My heart went cold at the thought of losing this memory, for it was the last moment of true happiness in my life. A few short weeks later, Lucifer would return to the village and destroy the lives of those two young lovers and those of everyone they knew. I sometimes comforted myself with the knowledge that at least Hamin had the recollection of that day to keep him warm in the bowels of Hell.

Nothing left.

"No..."

"Of course, you do not have to give me this memory." Beelzebub's smile was so wide I could see bits of his dinner trapped in his molars. "You know that Lucifer will not allow me to keep you here indefinitely. I'm sure that in the next few weeks, he will discover that you are here and insist that I release you. But I was under the impression that you were in something of a hurry."

I swallowed, considering the costs. Beelzebub was right; I could wait for Lucifer to free me, but demons did not regard the passage of time in the same way that humans did. It could be weeks or months before Lucifer found out where I was and insisted on my release. Even though I wasn't sure of the exact date, Sebastian had less than two weeks left before his contract came due. And even if Lucifer freed me in time, I wasn't sure that my mind could stand up to the barrage of damned souls for even a few days. So I had to choose which I valued more, a single memory or a man's soul. One moment of happiness or my sanity.

Never a choice.

When I put it like that to myself, the choice was clear. "All right." I looked the archdemon in the eyes, unwilling to let him have the satisfaction of seeing any doubt on my face. "All right. I accept the cost. Take the memory."

I closed my eyes and tried to hold onto as much of that memory as I could. I concentrated on the sight of Hamin's smile and the sound of my innocent laugh. I focused on everything my body was feeling, from my husband's lips on mine to the feel of the brick floor under my toes.

After only a few seconds, Beelzebub announced that the memory was gone. As he returned the globe to his pocket, I grasped at the bits of memory I had struggled so hard to hold onto. I could not remember a single aspect. I remembered that Beelzebub said he was taking a memory, and I knew that the sphere had shown me pictures of the day I told my husband we were expecting our first child. But if I had ever known what that scene was like, I could not recall it now. It was if it had simply faded away with time.

Lost for all time.

"I would like to go home now." My voice sounded hollow to my ears, and I felt as though I wanted to cry but could not remember the reason.

Still grinning, Beelzebub walked over to one of the sideboards, which grew until the doors were large enough for someone to walk through. The demon opened one and gestured that I should pass through. "So glad you could come to visit, Corinna. Please come again any time."

I did not even look at the demon as I left his lair to return to my world.

CHAPTER 11

THE DINER WAS BUSIER THAN usual the next day. At no point were all my tables empty, and at least once I had five tables filled. If this kind of traffic kept up, I was definitely going to need to hire a waitress. Oh, well, I would worry about that later. Like when I was done making daily trips to Hell.

About an hour after my last customer left and Madame Zarita shuffled out the door, the jukebox still played bitter breakup music. (Kelly Clarkson, "Since U Been Gone," which indicated Bedlam's state of mind. He had an irrational dislike of the first *American Idol* winner and excluded her from all playlists.) I finished wiping down the tables and washing the dishes. I added the dishwasher to the mental list of things I needed to take care of when I had finished trying to save Sebastian's soul. *And laundry, too,* I thought as I tossed my green drying towel into the overflowing basin behind the counter and made my way up my darkened staircase.

That next descent into Hell felt different from the others. As I moved toward the next archdemon, I did not feel the solidity of walls closing in around my body as it became corporeal. Phantom breezes blew my hair across my cheek, and the wind rustled the last of the dry brown leaves that clung to the branches of sturdy oak trees. Sticks and stems bit into my bare feet as I moved across the forest floor. A howl echoed through the woods, and when I turned toward it, I saw the outside of the gothic mansion in the distance, the full moon shining over its turrets.

As before, the scene shifted before me, from the ancient forest to the strangely deserted Hyde Park of a nineteenth century London season to the Amazonian jungle.

When the scene flickered to a lush green forest in Ancient Greece that I remembered far too well, I knew that I had entered the realm of the Harpy Queen, the leader of the Wild Hunt: the archdemon Lilith.

Lilith and I first met when I was living in the forest I now saw reflected in her domain, a short distance from a small village on the isle of Crete. I made my living dying wool, spinning it into yarn, and weaving it into blankets. I had finished my latest creation and traveled into the village to meet with a local farmer's wife named Irene who had promised to trade me a few weeks' worth of grain for my work.

"Thank you so much, Callidora." Irene admired the blanket for a moment and then set it aside. She leaned forward and whispered, "But I need to talk to you about what you've seen in the bones. Do you know? Will Methodius and I have a child at last?"

"I've told you before, I can't see the future." *Why is it that no matter where I go, no one believes that?*

"But you are blessed of Demeter. You must know something of what is to come!" *Surely the goddess must be angry with me to not have blessed us with a child. She is punishing me for being an inadequate wife.*

I laid my hand on hers. "You mustn't think that it is your fault. Demeter knows you are a good wife, and she will grant you a child in the proper time. You have only been married a year."

"I am sure you are right." Irene sighed and seemed about to say something further, but I held up a hand to stop her. I sensed a mind strong enough to be an angel's, somewhere in the town.

I turned to see a nattering crowd forming at the southern edge of the bustling marketplace. Irene and I moved to join the crowd. As I approached, I realized there were several demon minds up ahead, all of them dark and malevolent. A troupe of wild, leather-clad women emerged from the woods, with spears in their hands and longbows on their backs. The leader was taller and more beautiful than anyone the villagers had ever seen. Even I, who had seen many more people than they, was hard-pressed to recall a woman of such attractiveness. Her long, black hair fell in untamed curls down her back, and her copper skin was as clear as tempered bronze. The villagers could only see her glory, but I knew her black eyes and heartless soul revealed her to be a cohort of Mephistopheles and Lucifer, and the women who surrounded her to be her fellow fallen angels.

When she was sure every eye was upon her, the leader declared, "My name is Lilith, and these are my Amazon warriors. We have come to bestow an honor upon your village. My sisters and I shall select the strongest and wisest of your menfolk to lie with, and the female children born from these unions shall become part of our tribe and be raised as Amazons."

"Isn't it amazing?" Anthousa, the village gossip had come up behind Irene and me. "These warriors are favored of Artemis, and they have chosen to honor our village."

"Are you sure you should trust them?" I looked around me; the villagers' reactions seemed to match Anthousa's. I felt a pit form in my stomach. "After all, Artemis is a virgin huntress. Why would those she favors seek the men of this or any village?"

"You're jealous because you have no sons or husband to offer them."

I searched Anthousa's mind for any sign that she did not believe the words that came out of her mouth, but it was as if she had been placed under some kind of enchantment. I turned to Irene. "Surely you would not let Methodius lie with one of these women."

Irene blushed. "If he were so fortunate as for one of these women to favor him, I would not wish to stand in his way."

And so it went with all the people in the town. I tried with increasing desperation to convince the town to deny these women what they asked, but it was as if Lilith had cast a spell to which I was immune. And thus the women willingly let their husbands and sons couple with those Amazons, and many of the young girls even sought to join the strange band of women.

The harpies stayed in the village for seven days and seven nights, and during that time the village partook of almost ceaseless celebration. During nights of drunken debauchery, the townsfolk feasted upon foods they might better have saved for the coming winter. I tried to stay away so that I would not have to hear the vile thoughts of the demons, but my house was near enough to the village that I could not completely shut out the sounds of the revelry. I thought of leaving the town but felt that I had to remain, to lend what aid I could when whatever disaster Lilith planned came to pass. Each day I ventured out and urged those villagers whose trust I thought I had earned to cast those visitors out, but each day, my pleas were ignored.

On the fifth day, Lilith blocked my path back to my house, with five or six harpies flanking her. "What have we here, girls?"

"It looks boring." The speaker made a large mocking yawn. The other warrior women laughed.

"Oh, no. I think this is something very special. They say she is favored of the harvest goddess." Lilith turned to me. "Is that what you are? One of Keziel's little mice? A good God-fearing girl? No, I see that you are not. You are something quite more special than that. What is your name, girl?"

131

"I'm Callidora, and I would appreciate it if you would let me pass." My voice was quiet, but I allowed a hint of defiance to creep into my tone.

"Oh, but I have an offer for you. These humans here, they are worthless. The men are savages, and the women follow the path that Keziel set down for them, believing they must serve. But you, you are like I am, bound to the will of the Devil through no fault of your own. So I offer you what I have never offered a human: the opportunity to come join my hunt, my warriors, my harpies. You would not be just another human soul, but one of my favored riders. I cannot save you from Lucifer's service, but I can make it so you have some freedom."

I realized that, in her own twisted way, Lilith meant what she said, that she wanted to do me a favor. She felt trapped by God, by Lucifer, and by her own nature, none of which allowed her to seek a productive means of liberating herself.

Doesn't she see this is the only freedom we have? Lilith thought. *The power to strike back at our captors.*

But because I understood and pitied her did not mean I was willing to join her or that I would not do whatever I could do to stop her. "What if I did go with you? Would you be willing to let the people in this town go?"

When the warrior queen laughed, her harpies joined in. "Are you trying to bargain with me, little one? I seek to do you a favor, but it is no cost to me if you refuse. These people serve that which is abhorrent to me, and so they must be punished. Were you to come with me, you would understand that, in time. Are you sure you do not wish to join with us?"

Leave my home and hearth to be a harpy? Join them on their misbegotten quest to pillage decent society? "I beg you, do not hurt these people."

She scowled and waved her hand. "You begin to bore me now. I have already told you that they must be punished. Now be a good girl and run along home."

132

I did not return to the town until the eighth morning, and I only returned then because their mourning could not be ignored or denied. As I entered the town proper, the women gathered around the well, weeping and holding each other. Irene clutched Methodius's body, wrapped in the bloody remains of the blanket I had traded to her only a week before. In the early hours of the morning, Lilith and her Amazons had slain all the men with whom they had coupled and then rode off before the dawn.

It was inevitable that the people of the town would then turn on me, in the wake of this tragedy. After all, predicting a bad outcome was only one small step from causing it. And so the next night, I found myself disappearing into the woods as Lilith had while the women and few remaining men came with torches to burn my house.

I stood alone in Lilith's woods in Hell. I thought it unlikely that I would be able to find the exit by myself, but searching for it seemed like a better idea than standing there in the cold. I set off in the direction of the house, on the assumption that it was more likely to have a door than anything else in these woods.

No way out, said the souls of the damned, their voices fading in and out with the wind.

I walked for what felt like hours, but I was no closer to the house, and the moon maintained its same position in the sky. The trees shifted around me from Cretan plane trees to Asian ginkgoes to more common oaks and elms. I didn't see much in the way of wildlife, but if it were night in the forest, I suspected most would be asleep. With each step I took, I felt the sticks of the forest floor dig into my unprotected feet; and with each moment, the crush of the souls of Hell threatened to overpower my mind. At last, I could walk no more and sat down at the base of a nearby oak. I tried to remain conscious, but I had to close my eyes to relieve the pressure in my skull, and I fell into a slumber.

Never to wake.

As I slept, I dreamt of the harpies' return to the forest. The demons ran through the woods, some on horseback, some on foot. They stopped in a clearing and built up a fire. Some began beating drums and playing pipes, creating an unearthly music that seemed to pulse in time with the Hellscape. A few climbed up into the trees and crowed at the moon in a tribute to their queen. The rest danced around the fire, wild and uncontained, and eventually Lilith herself arrived to join in the dance. The music became louder and louder, until the sound overpowered the screams of the damned.

I woke to find Lilith standing over me, looking almost exactly as she had the first time I saw her. As she had been in the dream, she was dressed as the eternal huntress, clad in leather skinned from the hides of her victims. I glanced around; she was accompanied by a half dozen or so of her harpies. Unlike the mythic figures that bore the same name, Lilith's harpies were not half-woman, half-bird, but ordinary females with a black-eyed human form and a spirit form, like any other demon. The ones watching me were all dressed in the same manner as their leader, and their narrowed gazes said they hoped I would give them an excuse to tear me limb from limb.

"Hello, Callidora. Come to join my hunt?" She gave me a feral smile that suggested that she plotted ways to use me as her evening's entertainment.

"I'm afraid not, Lilith. I only seek passage out of your realm, if you would be so kind as to grant it to me."

The Harpy Queen shook her mane of dark curls and laughed. "Even if I were inclined to let you go—which I am not—appealing to my sense of kindness would do you no good. If you want kindness in Hell, you must seek out my sister Lethe, if you can stomach her cries. Here you will find only the cold, hard truth of the blade."

Only pain.

"Lilith, I have no interest in playing games with you." My words carried more bite than they would have, were I under less duress. "I came into your woods in error, and I would appreciate if you would tell me what you would like from me in exchange for revealing the door out."

"To reveal the door? I require nothing for that." She waved her hand.

I looked around for a door but did not see one. I raised my eyebrows.

No escape.

"No games, though? Well, that would not be any fun at all. You enter my forest uninvited and again refuse the honor of joining my hunt. It's only fair that you provide me with a little entertainment. Don't you think?"

I opened my mouth to respond, but she continued before I could answer, "The rules are simple. The door is somewhere in my woods, and if you can find and enter it, you are free to leave."

"So what's the catch?" *There has to be a catch.*

"Well, while you are searching for the door, the hunt will be pursuing you. If they catch you, you will have no choice but to remain here with us."

Suffer with us.

My heart beat faster. "That hardly seems fair." I kept my voice even. "You know that no mere mortal can outrun your hunt."

She harrumphed. "I suppose you are right, though you know that you are not just any mortal. But even you could not hope to defeat my warriors. I suppose I could give you a ten-minute head start, and perhaps a hint. Hmm... What would be a good hint? How about this: You can never walk into or out of my forest."

"That's it?" *That can't be the hint.*

No chance.

"Yes, I think I have given you a sporting chance. Also,

your ten minutes started when I gave you the riddle, so you will probably want to get going."

I turned and moved deeper into the woods.

Run! screamed the animal part of my brain. I started out at a jog. I wanted to put as much distance between me and the hunt as I could. I peered into the darkness, trying to recognize the trees around me. I needed to learn their pattern so that I would know if I passed the same area twice.

The forest shifted as I moved. At every turn, the trees stood in my way, as if aiding Lilith in her game. I dodged a Pennsylvania hemlock tree to find myself whipped in the face by a willow. Branches scratched my arms as I passed through what seemed to be a grove of olive trees, and then I found myself at the base of a massive sequoia.

Far from home.

As I ran, I thought about the clue. She had to be referencing the old riddle about how far one could walk into the woods. The answer was halfway, because after that, one would be walking out. *I tried to walk out of the woods when I first got here. I couldn't.*

A branch snapped somewhere to my left. My head whipped in that direction. My legs tangled in a branch on the ground. I toppled over, using my hands to break my fall. A sharp twig pierced my hand. I cried out with pain as I removed the object. I glanced at the scrapes on my hands and legs. They bled a little, but they could wait.

Coming to get you.

My breathing sped up. My lungs had been heated by the running, and the cold air hurt going in. I made an effort to slow my gasps. *In, out, in, out.*

If I can't walk into the woods, either, that must mean... *The door is in the center.* Yes, that made sense. If I started at the edge of a wood, I would always be walking toward an exit. But where was the center?

An evergreen shrub to my right started to rustle. I

jumped back as a bat emerged in my face. I covered my face with my hands. It flew off in to the night. As I looked up, I made out the shadows of a flock of birds against the full moon.

Forever night.

I placed my hand on a tree while I caught my breath. I felt something move under my fingers, then a sharp prick on my palm. I looked down and saw a wasp on my hand, and a dozen more rising from a hive I had disturbed. I screamed and waved my hands as the insects swarmed in my face. I took off at a breakneck pace through the trees. The wasps buzzed behind me. One stung my back; another, my side. I batted one away as it pierced my neck, and three more got me on my legs.

When I could no longer hear the angry swarm behind me, I reduced my speed, but I could not afford to stop. I took a calming breath and tried to focus on how to find the center of the forest. *It must be different in some way. Like the clearing in my dream. But which way is it?*

No way out.

I slowed so I could focus, but I couldn't allow myself to stop. I used every sense to seek a difference in the forest around me. Did I remember that birch from my dream? Was that treeless spot the beginning of a path? Could I smell the slightest hint of smoke on the breeze coming from that direction? *Yes. There.* That was the direction I needed to go.

I turned toward the clearing and picked up my pace. I stumbled once over a dead stump and nearly fell, but I righted myself and continued on. I dodged a slew of mismatched maples, pines, and cherry trees. After what seemed like forever but was likely only a moment or two, I found myself in the treeless clearing. But there was no door.

My breathing became even more labored than it had during my run, and my heart pounded against my rib cage.

It has to be here! If it's not, I'm going to be trapped with the harpies for who knows how long! I couldn't bear that.

I studied the base of every tree that faced the defoliated area. *What did she say?*

No release.

"You can never walk into or out of my forest." That was true. I hadn't *walked* into the forest. It had formed around me.

Maybe that was the answer. *Not walk. So maybe... climb?*

I looked up, but there were only trees, stretching as high as the eye could see. *Fall, then.*

My gaze landed on the bonfire pit in the clearing. I sprinted over. There, under the piles of charred wood and stone lay the outline of the door.

I breathed a sigh of relief, but as the air passed through my lips, a whoop sounded from inside the forest. The hunt had been released.

Never outrun them.

I grabbed a piece of burnt wood and threw it off the pit.

I heard a harpy laugh and imagined her feet pounding against the forest floor.

Coming for you now.

I pushed a pile of timber and stone away from the door. I felt the sharp prick of a splinter on my palm.

The vicious snarling of the harpy minds drew closer.

Closer and closer.

I heaved as much wood as I could off the portal out of Hell. Was it clear enough for me to open the door?

A glance over my shoulder showed me that the first harpy was running into the clearing.

Going to catch you.

I tugged at the door. It stuck. I screamed, the sound sticking in my throat.

I could almost feel the breath of the harpies on the back of my neck.

No retreat.

I tugged at door, harder than before. It opened. I jumped inside. As I fell and pulled the door closed, harpy fists hammered on the heavy wood, missing their chance to grab me and drag me back into Hell.

CHAPTER 12

I TUMBLED THROUGH THE ABYSS FOR a time that seemed interminable. When I stopped, I opened my eyes and lurched upward with a scream, as if I had hit the ground after falling in a dream. I took a moment to steady my breathing and reorient myself to my room.

There was light streaming through my window.

Ugh, late to open the diner again, I thought. *How long was I in Lilith's domain?*

I rolled out of bed. As I put pressure on the soles of my feet, they felt sore, as if I had been running barefoot through a real forest last night and not just a representation of one. One glance at my hands told me that I had the scrapes and puncture wounds from falling, as well. Mephistopheles had been right when he said that damage to my spirit in Hell would be reflected in my physical body.

I had just begun to process that discovery when Gabriel appeared in front of me. Much to my surprise, he grabbed my shoulders and pulled me into a hug.

"Cassia!" Relief flooded him. "You're all right! Thank the Lord!"

What prompted this? Not that I mind, but... Crap. He knows I was in Hell.

"Um, Gabriel?" My voice was muffled, as my mouth was crushed against his chest. "What's going on?"

He didn't loosen his grip on me. "You weren't here when I came by this morning. It was past opening time, and Dwayne and Madame Zarita were all set up without you. I came up to check on you, and you didn't respond when I called your name or shook you." *Light save me, I thought I'd lost her.*

I pulled away from him. "Well, I'm fine. But I really am running late, and I should get dressed so I can relieve Dwayne from having to cook and wait tables. I've been surprisingly busy this week." I turned and started making my bed, more out of a desire to hide the guilty expression that I felt sure I wore than out of any desire to fluff my pillow. *Please let me go. Don't ask about—*

Gabriel pulled me back to face him with a firm grip on my arm. "Cassia, you are not fine. I've seen you sleep before, and it's never been like that." He glanced down at my hand. "And you've got all kinds of scrapes and bruises. I don't know what's happening, but I believe you should see a physician."

I laughed, but it sounded false even to my ears. "I'm pretty sure there aren't doctors specializing in people like me. But you really don't have to worry, because really, I am totally and completely fine. I was just about to tend to those." *Drop it. Drop it. Please, just drop it.*

Unfortunately, my powers have always tended more toward the reception of emotions than their transmission. "Wait a minute." Gabriel's eyes narrowed in suspicion. "You know what happened. You're just not telling me."

A little piece of my heart broke to hear the distrust in his voice. I remembered how, when I first met him, he couldn't comprehend dishonesty. "Can't you trust me to take care of myself, Gabriel?"

I tried to move past him to get clothes from my closet, but he took hold of my arm with a grasp that, while not sufficient to injure me, was enough to hold me in place.

"Was it Bedlam? Did he come back and do something to you?"

My mouth dropped open at the suggestion. "What? No! Bedlam would never hurt me! How could you even think that?"

"Cassia, he's a demon. Demons hurt people." Though his tone was not unkind, he felt no reticence in making such a declaration. I had always known that he was wary of Bedlam, but I had never before realized that he actually considered the demon an enemy. "He even made you cry the other day. Don't pretend he didn't."

"Yes, he made me cry. So what?" I bristled and wrenched my arm out of his grasp, barely even noticing the pain it caused. "We had a fight. He hurt my feelings. That happens with friends sometimes. Besides, it's not like I have a lot of friends to choose from." *And now I'm picking a fight with my only other friend. If he leaves, I'll be totally alone. But I can't let him think that Bedlam would hurt me.*

Michael was right, Gabriel thought. *I'm not doing any good down here, getting caught up with demons.*

I was so surprised that I forgot to act as though I found it rude to eavesdrop on people's thoughts. "What? You've been spending time with Michael again? I thought I recognized the smell of crazy angel logic."

"Crazy angel logic? Thinking that demons are evil is not crazy!"

I crossed my arms. "It is if you apply it the way you did, like some kind of all-encompassing label. Like there's some kind of demonic syllogism: 'Everything a demon does is evil. Bedlam is a demon. Therefore, everything Bedlam does must be evil.' You know as well as I do that nothing is that absolute. Or at least, I thought you did!"

His blue eyes flashed with a degree of anger that I had never before seen from him. "Well, excuse me for being worried about you! The next time that Michael tells me that you're involved in some major disruption in the balance, I'll ignore whatever dangers you decide to subject yourself to."

"I'm involved in whatever has Keziel so worried?" I snapped my fingers, putting the pieces together. "That must have been why Mephistopheles seemed so pleased..."

"Mephistopheles!" Gabriel grabbed hold of both my arms. "When did you— *Why* did you see Mephistopheles?"

"Okay, now don't get upset." *No chance of that now.* "But I might have taken a trip to Hell..."

"What? Why? How? Why?"

"Um, which question do you want me to answer first?" He didn't seem inclined to answer that, so I told him briefly about how I made the journey through the hellhole in my kitchen.

Gabriel spoke through clenched teeth. "So what you're telling me is that when I found you this morning, you were in Hell talking to Mephistopheles?"

"Um. Not exactly." A smart part of my brain was yelling at me to lie, to pretend that I only went to Hell the one time, but no one has ever accused me of putting too much interest in my own self-preservation. "Last night I was talking to Lilith."

"You went to Hell twice?"

"Um. Three times. And I have to go at least once more."

"Cassia, why?" Gabriel shook me. "Why could you possibly need to go to Hell one time, let alone four? Do you have any idea how dangerous that is?"

I took a deep breath. "Yes, Gabriel, of course I know how dangerous Hell is. The question is, do you know how dangerous it is for me? I can't die, and Lucifer won't let any of his angels hold me against my will for very long. The worst thing that could happen is that I get stuck in Hell for a few months."

"Cassia, that's a pretty bad 'worst thing.'"

"True, and it wouldn't be my first choice for an extended vacation. But so far, the archdemons have all let me go with relatively little hassle." *And let's not talk about the Abyss full of screaming souls.* "Um... Gabriel? Can you please let go of my arms? You're hurting me."

What? Hurting her? He took his hands away from me and stared at them as if he did not recognize them as

143

part of himself. Then he looked at me as if I were just as foreign. "But, Cassia, I don't understand. Why do you need to talk to the archdemons? And why do you have to go to Hell to do it?"

I sighed and continued my trip to my closet, as much for an excuse to get out from under Gabriel's reproachful stare as to pick out something to wear. "It's not for me. It's for Sebastian."

Gabriel's head turned to follow me as I walked past. "Who's Sebastian?"

I clarified that Sebastian was the damned man he had accidentally sent my way. "He's going to go to Hell in a few days if someone doesn't do something. And he doesn't deserve to be there. I have to find Azrael and convince her to let him go." *Or at least I have to try.* I pulled a green cardigan and a denim skirt off of their hangers.

I tried not to look at Gabriel but couldn't help but glance at his regretful expression. "I know it's sad, but he knew what he was doing when he made that choice. God gave people free will so that they could make these choices for themselves. We need to respect that."

I turned around and pulled open my top dresser drawer. "You don't understand. I have met so many people who have sold their souls. Over the years, so many of them have found their way to me, begging for a way out. You know this, because you have seen me turn them away, again and again. I wouldn't have helped them even if I could have. Those souls were so bogged down by their own choices that even if I could have overturned their contracts, there was no way to redeem them." I took out underwear and a tank top from their respective piles.

Tears began to form at the corners of my eyes. I tried to shut the drawer, but it stuck, so I tried again, harder this time. *James. Gladys. Marcus. William. My village elders.* A list of all the souls I had failed to save ran like a litany through my head. "But this one is different, Gabriel. This one does not belong in Hell. He has only ever acted with love and faith and compassion and all the things that you keep saying your God wants. He's made thousands of choices to be good in a world where it's really hard to be good, and it's not fair that this one choice matters more than any other."

"Okay, Cassia. Okay. I understand."

I turned back to face him and clutched my clothing to my chest. *You think you mean that, but you don't. No matter what, you won't see that the world is not fair, that everything is not part of some large divine plan. How can I explain to you that I can't accept this?*

Gabriel wiped the tears from under one of my eyes, then rested his palm on my face. "I'm so sorry. This is all my fault. I should have known better than to tell that girl about you. I forget how hard it is for you. I see people suffering and know that God allows everything to happen as it should. I don't know if I could do that, if I felt their pain like you do."

"Oh, Gabriel." He was standing so close to me. I couldn't remember a time when he had ever stood next to me like that, his hand on my cheek, his eyes looking into mine. I wondered what he would do if I took the tiniest step forward and reached up to kiss him. "It's not your fault. You were trying to help."

He smiled at me, but his eyes and mind were still full of sorrow. "I know, but I hurt you, and I'm sorry for that. Just promise me that you'll stop this going to Hell nonsense."

I took a deep breath and stepped away from his hand. "I can't promise that."

He was so shocked that it took him a moment to remember to drop his hand. "Why? I know you want to help him, but you're putting yourself in danger. No one wins if you save this man's soul but sacrifice your own."

I walked past him again, back towards my bathroom. "You know it doesn't work that way. You can't measure one soul's value in terms of other people's. One soul does not have the value of one other soul or a hundred other souls. Each one is unique and invaluable."

"Exactly. And I cannot bear to lose your unique and invaluable soul."

I put my clothes on top of the sink and flipped the light switch on, and the fan began to whir. "My soul's value was determined a long time ago. Ten people's souls paid for my life, and there isn't a day that goes by that I don't hate myself for the suffering I caused them."

Gabriel had come up behind me and stood in front of me again. "Cassia, that wasn't your fault! I know that Michael has done his best to convince you that you're somehow to blame, but you were never to blame! You can't hold yourself culpable for other people's choices!"

I glared up at him. "I 'can't hold myself culpable'? Gabriel, the entire universe holds me culpable! There is a reason I can't see the Pearly Gates. The fair and just world that you want to believe in has long since judged me and found me wanting."

He met my stare with equal fervor. "That is not true. You say that you are sure this Sebastian does not belong in Hell. Well, I am just as certain that you do not. You are not here as part of some evil plan of Lucifer's. You are here because the world needs you." His voice hitched. "Because I need you."

I gazed up at him, and try as I might, I could not stay angry with him. I wanted to believe what he was saying, that he needed me the way I needed him. I wanted to forget everything that was happening and stand on my tiptoes and press my lips to his. The way he looked at me right now, I could almost believe that he would respond in kind.

But what would that even mean? He said he needed me, but he was talking about someone who did not exist. Some version of me that could stand by while an innocent man was sent to Hell. Some girl who hadn't been damned by the actions of others, long before he met her.

"You don't mean that." I felt tears once again stream down my cheeks.

He stepped forward and held my face in both of his hands. "I do, Cassia." There was no doubt in his mind. "Please. Please don't do this. I cannot bear to lose you."

I looked up into his blue eyes, and he looked so earnest that I wanted to give him whatever he wanted, so that he would always keep looking at me that way. But I thought about Sebastian and about what he would suffer, and... "I have to."

A wave of sadness washed over him as he dropped his hands and backed away from me. "I can't watch you do this."

He disappeared.

CHAPTER 13

I STOOD THERE FOR A LONG time, letting the tears fall down my face, but eventually I made myself shower and dress. I hated upsetting Gabriel, but as I had told him, I wasn't going to let that stop me from helping Sebastian. I resolved that if I made it through the situation intact, I would find a way to make it up to the angel. He couldn't stay mad at me forever.

And if I didn't make it through, as he was so concerned would be the case, then I would have other things to worry about.

Dwayne and Madame Zarita had opened the diner for me, but if there were any customers to notice my absence, they were gone by the time I went downstairs. I expected to be feeling even more miserable that day than I had the day before. After all, I had since managed to drive away both of my friends, and the jukebox had moved onto more obscure break-up songs like Magnetic Fields's "I Thought You Were My Boyfriend." But I suffered through well enough, and after I closed the diner for the day, I trudged up the stairs to make another journey into Hell.

As I pulled my way out of the nothingness toward the domain of the fourth archdemon, the first sensation I experienced was that of a hideous, high-pitched scream. There were not words to describe how unspeakable the noise was. I could compare it to a hundred children scratching their fingernails down blackboards or a thousand first-year violin students striving to make the worst sounds they could imagine, but these descriptions could not even begin to approach the unspeakable wretchedness that assaulted my ears. The sound merged with the voices of the souls in Hell, adding a discordant descant to their litany. As soon as I recognized my hands, I pressed them against the sides of my head, but the gesture was insufficient to shield myself from the worst of the ghastly keening.

Keeping my hands over my ears, I looked around at my surroundings. I appeared to be inside a chapel, attached to the same mansion in which I had found Mephistopheles and Beelzebub. However, while the previous two areas I visited had been clean and orderly, the chapel was in appalling disrepair. All of the stained glass windows were shattered, and the faded fragments were littered all over the floor. Half of the pews were swathed in dusty sheets, and wax-covered candelabras lay fallen on the floor. As I gazed around, the scene shifted to other scenes of religious worship—the temple of Isis where I met Bedlam, a shrine to Demeter in Greece, and even the Catholic church down the street from the diner. All were in poorer condition than when I had last seen them. I looked up and found gaps in the ceiling, and through them, I saw the source of the wailing: dozens of demons, floating through the night sky.

I spotted what seemed like a pile of cloth in front of the altar and walked down the center aisle to examine it more closely. As I approached, the rags seemed to be moving slightly, and I worried that the room had somehow become rat-infested as well as dusty.

I heard a noise coming from the same direction and realized that the movement was a chest heaving with gut-wrenching sobs. When I was close enough, I automatically reached out to smooth the white-blond hair on her shoulder, but as soon as I touched her, she lifted up her head and let out a scream that put the cries of her banshees to shame. As soon as she looked at me, I knew that I was staring into the black eyes of the archdemon Lethe, leader of the banshees who glided through the air above our heads.

It took me a moment to notice that the sounds emerging from Lethe's mouth were not empty screeches and were, in fact, meaningful phonemes. "Who are you? What are you doing here?"

"I'm Carrie." She looked so small and pitiable, the tiny blond girl looking up at me with tears streaming down her face. She was one of the rulers of Hell, but looking at how sad she was, I couldn't resist reaching out to her. "Can I... Can I help you?"

She let out her loudest scream yet, and a burst of wind blew me across the chapel and into the wall. I was dizzy for a moment, and when my vision cleared, she had stood up and was walking toward me.

"Can you help me?" She let out another ear-shattering wail. "No one can help me! I have been forsworn by everyone I ever loved."

No help, whispered the souls of the damned, and the wails of the banshees drifting above my head echoed the tidings.

I considered getting up but decided it was better not to startle her with any sudden movements, thereby getting myself thrown against a wall again. Based on my level of dizziness, I suspected that I already had a concussion. "I'm sorry. I didn't mean to disturb you. If you could open the door for me, I'll be on my way."

"Do you know who I am?" She seemed not to have heard me. I was not even sure that she knew I was there anymore. She didn't look at me, and given her apparently loose grip on sanity, she could well have forgotten me or thought I was an illusion. "I am Lethe, Betzalel, once beloved of Michael the archangel, once one of the most powerful angels in the Heaven. No more." She punctuated her words with another scream and then snapped her head around to look directly at me. "Would you like to hear my tale?"

If I wanted to get out of there, I was going to have to calm Lethe enough that she would open the door out, so it was important that I answer her correctly. In most circumstances, I would think that she was offering to tell me her story because that was what she wanted, but she had reacted badly to an offer of help and might feel similarly about another attempt at kindness. Since I had no powers over demons in Hell, I could not look into her mind and see what she might feel.

Only chaos.

I opted for encouraging her to talk to me, if only because any type of engagement increased the possibility of her remembering I was there. "Yes, please. Tell me your tale."

She seemed pleased and moved closer to me, crouching down so that she could meet my gaze. "No one ever wants to hear my tale." Her eyes were bright, like those of a child desperate for attention. "'Be quiet, Lethe,' they say to me. 'Stop your wailing, woman!' No one understands my pain!" She screamed again.

No one cares.

"I'm here, and I want to hear your tale." I said it in part to calm the crying child, but I did want to hear what had happened to Lethe. It had always seemed unfathomable to me that Michael could love anyone, much less a demon.

She stood up and walked a bit away from me. Suddenly, she was no longer a child but a world-weary old woman. "I was beautiful once, in Heaven. I remember being there, being glorious. And I had my Michael there, by my side." She sighed, momentarily overcome by the happy memory, and for a moment, I saw the part of her that was the benevolent angel.

She snapped her head around to me again, with the petty, manipulative demon part of her in control. "Do you know my Michael?"

I was again unsure of the correct answer and therefore elected to tell the truth. "Yes, I have met him." I tried to keep my voice as neutral as possible. I knew from my experiences with Bedlam that spurned demons tended to react badly when someone criticized the angels that they still loved, no matter how hateful those angels were.

She smirked at me, again a child with a love of secrets. "You don't like him. I can tell." She turned away from me again, still smiling. "That's all right. Lots of people don't like him. 'How can you love him, Lethe?' they would ask. 'He's so hard and cold and unyielding. And you are not any of those things.' But they could not see how I needed those things, like he needed me. Michael helped me be strong, and I helped him see the value of mercy. I knew that we were meant to be together forever and ever and ever..."

Cold forever.

She was silent for so long that I began to wonder if she remembered what she was doing. I couldn't tell which part of her was in control—the angel or the demon—and I was about to break the silence when the demon returned. "I didn't do anything wrong, you know. Not really. I only did what I had to do. You know that, right?"

As I tried to determine the proper response to that, she answered her own question. "No, of course you don't. Michael runs the universe now, and he has cast me as the villain."

"He doesn't tell the story at all. I think it's too painful."

She smiled with a level of cruel satisfaction greater than any I had ever seen. "Then he suffers. He suffers like I do. He deserves to suffer. He deserves to burn for eternity for what he did to me."

Burn in Hell.

She screamed again, and I realized that I needed to get her back on track or I might well be stuck there, listening to the noise, until Lucifer came to get me. "So tell me. Tell me what he did to you."

"I fought for Heaven." Again she became the tired old woman. "I fought for God and Michael, and I helped subdue

Lucifer." She looked at me, and the demon peered out of those eyes. "I didn't have to, you know. Azrael didn't. She said she was the angel of love and, as such, could not participate in a war. Raziel wouldn't have fought if he had still been around. Maybe. And me, I am the angel of mercy. To harm my fellows, it went against everything that I believed in. But I did it anyway. But it wasn't enough. Why wasn't it enough?"

Never enough.

"I don't know," I answered.

Suddenly she was crouched beside me. "You do know!" Her eyes were as hard and cold as any of her fellow archdemons'. "I know who you are, little girl! Lucifer's pet. Bedlam's keeper. You think you're so innocent, but you hold all our secrets. You know like Lucifer knows. You know because you are crawling around in my head!" Her screams became louder and higher as she stood up and clutched her hands to her temples.

My head ached, from some combination of my injury and the wailing of both the banshees and the damned, and I needed to do something to diminish the yelling. "I'm not. I have no powers here. I couldn't see inside your head even if I wanted to."

Never understand.

She cocked her head to the side, considering me. "Okay," she concluded with all the capriciousness of a child. "I believe you."

She rolled her head around a few times. "When it was all over, when Michael had won, he called us all in, one at a time, to face judgment, even those who had fought at his side. God would tell him who had been true and who had fallen. And Michael had to do it alone. I begged him to let me help him, to take some of the burden, but he said I could not. I felt so badly for him then. How could he bear it, casting out the angels who had been his brothers? I ached at the thought and believed he must feel the same.

But I forgot that he was not like me. 'He's hard and cold and unyielding,' everyone told me, but I didn't believe, not really, not until that day."

No mercy.

"One by one, he called us all in, starting at the bottom and moving up to the top. I was near the end. For then, once, I was glorious and powerful, and I was not worried, not for me. I knew that no matter what, my Michael would not harm me. I pitied them, pitied the ones whose screams I heard as they were cast upon the flaming sword. Then it was my turn."

"Michael smiled at me first, smiled as he always did when he saw me, *me* who would always be by his side. But then he stopped, and I didn't understand. He grabbed my arm, and he yelled, 'What did you do?'"

"'Nothing!' I said. I told him nothing, but he knew the truth. That I'd known, even before the war. I'd known it was coming, and I promised—had to promise—Lucifer that if it all ended badly, I would help. I would not let Michael cast them out. I would plead for mercy. 'I had to plead for mercy,' I told him. 'It's who I am—all I am.'"

Never mercy.

"He didn't understand, my Michael. He said I could have prevented everything, all the suffering, if I had warned someone of Lucifer's plans. He said that God had ordered me cast out. And I told him he did not have to obey this one time. He could let me stay. God would understand love. But he said, 'Azrael's gone, too.' And he pulled out his sword, and I said I wouldn't go. I tried to flee, but he struck me with his flaming sword. My Michael struck me down, and I woke up here, and here I've stayed."

She dropped to her knees and crawled over to me again. "You see, don't you?" She stared at me with widened eyes, pleading with me to understand. For a moment, she laid bare—to me and to herself—the truth of what she was, and more than anything, she wanted me to tell her that things

154

were different than they were. "How I had to promise to help Lucifer. How I've had to do everything I've done ever since. All the people in the world, they believe in their God and their love, and I have to tell them that it isn't like that. They have to know that their fears, their darkest doubts—these are what will come to pass. Heaven has no mercy for them. No mercy, no love, no hope." Again she began her high-pitched keening, a lament for the life she had lost.

No mercy. No love. No hope.

I let her cry for a time. It had likely been a long while since she had made herself face the truth of what had happened that day. I imagined that she preferred to live in the hazy fog of her own broken mind rather than face the world for what it was.

After a while, I realized that the only screams were the ones high above me. Lethe was staring at me, curiously. "Why are you here, little Carrie pet?" The conniving archdemon cocked her head to the side, as if considering ways that she could use my presence to her advantage. "You are not dead, for you are not as hopelessly abandoned as I am. The Morning Star looks out for you still. You are not supposed to be here."

I worried that if I told her the truth, that I had come in error, that she would resent it and refuse to let me leave. Her grip on sanity was so tenuous that I could not count on her to realize that Lucifer would not want her to hold me indefinitely. I also hesitated to lie to her, in part for the same reason and in part because I so rarely bothered to lie that I could not immediately think of a plausible one. "I did not mean to come here. I was searching for Azrael's domain."

All a mistake.

The plotting of the demon was replaced with the sorrow of a neglected child. "Of course you did not come for me. No one ever comes for me."

155

"But I am glad I came. I'm grateful that I was able to hear your story."

She gave me a little smile. "The door is over there." She pointed at a portal that had opened behind the altar at some point. "I could let you go, I suppose, but... no, I think I must ask something of you. There must be a price." She considered again. "I told you a story, so you must tell me a story."

Part of me wanted to run to the door and hope I got through it before she could stop me, but I have never been able to ignore the needs of someone suffering right in front of me. Besides, I did not want to leave myself in the debt of an archdemon. "Okay. What kind of a story?"

Only suffering.

She leaned forward and rested her head on her hands. "You know my Michael. It has been so long since I have seen him. Please, can you tell me of him? Anything, anything at all."

My heart went out to her as she made that simple request, but I didn't know what story I could tell about Michael that would satisfy her. Were she human, a tale of how her former lover had never been worth her love might have been appropriate, but Bedlam could not stand to hear a word against his precious Keziel, and I doubted that Lethe would be any different. And so I began.

In the 1790s, I lived in London, and Bedlam dragged me to the Assembly Room at Almack's a few evenings every month during the Season, though I had a hard time convincing him to follow all of society's rules.

"Ooh, those people look interesting." Bedlam pointed toward a couple on the other side of the room. "Let's go introduce ourselves."

I pushed his hand down and gave apologetic looks to the couple next to us, whose expressions and minds demonstrated dismay for his flagrant gesture. "How many times do I have to tell you that we can't just walk up to people and start talking to them? They're weird about that kind of thing here."

"And how many times do I have to tell you that I don't care? Pick out their names from their heads and pretend we were introduced last week." He started walking in their direction.

I grabbed the arm of his blue waistcoat and pulled him back. "Only if you promise to not go making up a dowry for me again."

Bedlam laughed. "That was hysterical. I should tell them how much you're actually worth. Every cad in London would want to dance with you."

"And then who would you dance with? None of the ladies would dance with someone to whom they haven't been properly introduced."

"You raise a valid point, as ever." He tugged at his cravat. "When is the dancing going to start, anyway? I'm bored of all this pointless mingling."

A strong mind entered the Assembly Room, and I let out a curse, once again to the horror of the couple beside us. Bedlam frowned at me, and I directed him toward a dark-complexioned woman approaching the people Bedlam had wanted to meet. "Lilith."

Bedlam scowled. "What's she doing here?"

I shrugged. "I don't know, but maybe she can introduce you to those people."

Bedlam shuddered. "No thanks. Any friend of Lilith's is no friend of mine. But it's got to be killing her to be in that prim getup. I can't let that go without comment."

He strode toward her, and I had no choice but to traipse after him.

"... really need to return to Paris, if you want to find your cousin," Lilith was saying.

"Oh, I long to see Cecile, to help her escape." Her accent

gave away her nationality. "But it is so dangerous. We would surely be risking the guillotine."

"I have just come from France." Lilith put her hand on the woman's arm. "It is not nearly as dangerous as it was." *Mainly because they've already hacked off the heads of most of the nobles left there. I need a fresh infusion of aristocracy to decapitate, and you will do nicely.*

I wanted to intervene and tell the couple not to return to France, under any circumstances. I had almost worked up the courage to do so when another angel mind appeared in the room, and for once, his anger was not directed at me. I turned to see Michael dressed in contemporary fashion but looking thoroughly disheveled and carrying his flaming greatsword. He pushed the crowd aside as he made his way toward us.

I turned to see Lilith, but she was moving through the crowd to the window. Her hunt might have been superhumanly fast, but on her own in ball-appropriate attire, she was no match for Michael's speed. He caught up to her as she reached the window and struck at her with the sword. She crashed through the glass and then disappeared as his fiery blade sent her to Hell.

The *beau monde* gaped at the archangel, unable to comprehend what had happened.

Bedlam broke the silence. He clapped his hands and cried out, "That was amazing! Do it again!"

Michael glared at him and held up his sword. "I only see one other demon in the room. Are you sure you want a repeat performance?"

Bedlam held up his hands in surrender, still grinning. "Hey, I haven't killed anyone in France since... before it was even France! I'm only here for the music. And the pudding."

Michael cringed and pinched the bridge of his nose. "You know what? Fine. Enjoy your pudding. I have another archdemon to find." And then he dematerialized.

"And that is the story of how Michael stopped some of the major demon-induced aspects of the French Revolution."

I had expected Lethe to interrupt me during the story, at least with the periodic wail or moan, but she sat in rapt silence for the entire time. Even the banshees floating above the chapel had abated their shrieks somewhat, calmed by the contentment of their leader.

"That is my Michael." Tears formed at the corners of her eyes. "So brave and strong, in spite of everyone and everything." Then she began to wail again, and her keening for all she had lost was echoed a hundredfold by the banshees.

All is lost.

It would be some time before she regained enough self-control to speak again, and I thought it best that I be gone by then. Hoping that I had done more good than harm in telling the tale, I quietly stood and walked through the exit she had provided.

CHAPTER 14

I HAD A HORRIBLE HEADACHE WHEN I returned to my body, and was now almost positive that I had a concussion. If Bedlam had been around, I would have had him wake me up during the night to make sure my pupils weren't dilated, but in his absence, I decided to chance an uninterrupted night's rest. One advantage to being immortal was that you could be pretty sure you wouldn't die in your sleep.

I awoke and opened the diner on time the next morning. Madame Zarita was back in her booth, and I had a customer, a boy with hair of a particularly unpleasant shade of yellow who ordered a rare steak with tomato juice. I was standing behind the counter waiting for him to finish when Sebastian walked in.

"Hi, Carrie." He glanced at the jukebox, which, after seventy-two hours straight of playing different break-up songs, was starting to grow desperate. Currently, it was playing the scene from *La Bohème* wherein Colline sings farewell to his coat. "It plays opera?"

I pulled a mug out from under the counter, assuming that he would want some coffee. "It plays whatever Bedlam wants it to. One week it played nothing but Indian mourning music, over and over. Be grateful for the opera."

"So, Bedlam." He looked at the stool upon which he had last seen my friend sit. "Is he really...?"

I poured a cup of coffee and slid it over to him. "A demon? Yes, but he's not so bad. I mean, technically, yes, he is a fallen angel, but he does his best to be good. Most of the time."

"Wow." He sat on one of the schools and took a sip of the coffee. "I mean, I guess I knew before. I sold my soul to one and everything, but I guess it's hard to fathom demons walking around the earth."

I shrugged. "There are angels too, if it makes you feel any better."

"Really?" It did seem to cheer him some. "What are angels like?"

"Honestly? Mostly self-righteous and irritating."

He smiled, then took another few sips of coffee. "So you're probably wondering what I'm doing here." I nodded at him. "Well, it's Tuesday now, and my contract is coming due on Saturday, which means I have fewer than five days left to spend on Earth. I've been trying to spend as much time with my family as possible, and I plan to spend the rest of the week with them. But the thing is, I need a break. It's so hard to pretend to be cheerful and normal around them when I know I'm going to be gone soon. Felicity knows, but she's angry at me about it, so that's not much of a comfort. I want to spend a day with someone who knew what I was going through and wouldn't judge me. And the only person I could think of like that was you. So I was wondering if you wanted to hang out with me today."

I opened my mouth to answer, but he continued before I could say anything. "I totally understand if you don't want to. I mean, you don't know me or anything, and I guess you have your diner to run. Plus, I was going to do some things I like to do in the city—you know, for the last time—and I would understand if you thought that was boring. I figured it wouldn't hurt to ask."

His request surprised me. It had been a long time since someone human had wanted to spend time with me for the pleasure of my company and not the insights I provided.

"Well, I need to wait until my customer goes," I said,

nodding at the yellow-haired boy, who was still working his way through the steak. "But I don't have that many customers, so I can close for the day without a problem. Dwayne will probably be overjoyed to get the day off, as long as I still pay him." I smiled at Sebastian, and much of his nervousness abated. "I could use a day off. I don't remember the last time I had one. Do you want something to eat while you are waiting?"

"Actually, I would love some bacon and scrambled eggs. If you don't mind." I sent his order back to Dwayne and poured him an orange juice.

Sebastian sat on a stool. "So of all the things you could be doing, why run a diner?"

I shrugged and slid his juice over to him. "I don't know where I had the idea. In the past, I've always worked for other people, but one day I just decided I wanted my own place. And a diner seemed so wonderfully normal. I love being able to spend time in my own space, where no one can kick Bedlam out if he stays too long."

"I can see that." Sebastian's food came out soon thereafter, and by the time he was done eating and I had washed his dishes, the diner was empty again, except for Madame Zarita, and she seemed pleased to be able to spend the day with her grandchildren. I switched the sign to "Closed" and ventured outside.

Feeling the breeze that hit me, I realized that it had been several weeks since I left the diner—for somewhere other than Hell, at least. I used to go out all the time, but I had recently been in a slump. There wasn't much to see on my block of brick-faced houses and businesses. The one-way street was lined on both sides with parked cars, and the unpleasant smell of exhaust fumes wafted through the air. We passed a few other pedestrians on the street, and Sebastian led me to where he had found a spot to park.

"So what are we doing today?" I climbed into his black sedan. I didn't have a car and had never learned to drive one. When I needed to go somewhere public transportation couldn't access, Bedlam provided the car.

Sebastian grinned at me. "It's a surprise."

I didn't see what good it did him to surprise me on his special day, but I decided to go along with it. "Do I get a hint?"

He thought for a moment. "How do you feel about hearts?"

"Um... fine for Valentine's, but I'm not going to wear little ones all over my clothes."

He laughed. "No, I meant the organ, the thing that beats in your chest."

"Oh." I considered his question. "I never really thought about it. For most of my life, the heart was considered to have the functionality of the brain. This concept of the heart as a blood-pumping muscle is rather unromantic, in comparison."

He glanced at me in astonishment, and I suspected he would have stared if he hadn't had to keep his eyes on the road. "How old are you, anyway? I mean... you just..."

I laughed at him. "It's okay. I gave up being sensitive about my age a long time ago. I stopped aging when I was about sixteen, I think. We didn't keep track of dates then like we do now. I guess I look older than that, since sixteen was a lot older back then. I was old enough to be married and have a child. As for when I was born, I'm not entirely sure. Most of the historical markers that you would know were identified in retrospect, and I wasn't near them at the time. But I believe it was somewhere in ancient Mesopotamia."

"That... is a very long time ago."

"It is." I glanced over at him; he was hiding it well, but the conversation was making him uncomfortable. "I'm creeping you out, aren't I?"

"It's not that. I just can't even imagine living that long. I mean, cognitively, yes, I can know that you've been alive for thousands of years, but I can't really imagine what it must be like."

"I understand." I turned my head to look out the window at the cars lining the side of the street. "Sometimes I look ahead, at all the time I'm going to have left, and realize that it's infinitely longer than what I've already lived, and it terrifies me. But I think I've been alive for so long that the idea of not having that—the idea of actually dying— terrifies me even more." We were silent for a few minutes. "So tell me about yourself and your life."

He shrugged as he turned the car left, onto another narrow one-way street. "Not too much to tell. I was born and raised in Philadelphia by a good Catholic family, with my younger brother and sister. I went to college at Villanova, where I majored in Sociology and Spanish. I was going to try to go on to law school; I wanted to be a public defender or work for Legal Aid. But then Felicity got sick, so there wasn't money for it. I figured I wouldn't be around to finish, anyway."

Sebastian drove us to a location on the Franklin Parkway. The signs said we were at the Franklin Institute. I had heard of it, I thought. It was some kind of science museum.

I felt an unexpected thrill to be going somewhere new. I must have been more bored with the diner than I realized.

"Come on!" Sebastian grabbed my hand and dragged me further into the museum. We came to a stop in front of something that looked like an enormous red plastic human heart, with a line of people coming out of a large purple blood vessel.

"Wow, that... is a giant heart," I said.

Still holding my hand, Sebastian pulled me to the end of the line. "I know it's lame, but we used to come here all the time when I was a kid. It's a learning tool. You move through the heart and lungs the way a blood cell would, and it tells you where you are, each step of the way."

As we moved further up the line, I heard the amplified sound of a heartbeat coming from the opening in front of us. "Okay."

Sebastian squeezed my hand and grinned at me. "You have to get into it! You can be a red blood cell, because you work at a diner and provide people with food, like the red blood cells carry oxygen to feed the body. I'm going to be a white blood cell and fight off infection!"

I agreed, and he pulled me through the line of people entering the opening in the side of the giant model heart. Sebastian's excitement was infectious, and I found myself laughing along as he described to me which part of the heart I was in and when I was supposed to pretend that I was obtaining oxygen from the lungs. "Again!" he cried when we emerged, and we got back in line to once again pretend we were blood cells being pumped through the body. After we went through about five times, some of the people were gaping at us, at the laughing couple who seemed a little old to be enjoying the heart quite that much.

I leaned over to catch my breath. "Where to next?"

When Sebastian didn't answer, I looked up at him. His gaze followed a young couple with two children, standing near the entrance to the heart. The little girl seemed afraid to go in, and her father picked her up and reassured her in a soothing voice.

That was supposed to be me, thought Sebastian. *I was going to bring my kids here.*

I rubbed his shoulder, but I didn't know what to say.

Next, we drove to the Wissahickon Valley Park. "We're going to walk along the Forbidden Drive, by the creek," Sebastian said as we got out of the car.

"Oh." I looked down at my kitten-heeled sandals with some concern. "I don't think I have the right kind of shoes for that, and my feet are sore from some walking I was doing the other day."

He looked stricken. "I hadn't even noticed. It didn't occur to me that today might have a dress code."

He was reconsidering the trip, and I hated to spoil his day like that. "I think I'll be all right. If we don't go too fast, my feet should be fine."

He let out a sigh of relief. "Okay. But let me know if your feet hurt too badly, and we'll stop or turn back."

"Your family came here a lot?" I asked as we started down the trail.

He shook his head. "Mostly my friends. I had a girlfriend in high school, Nicole, who loved to go walking or hiking anywhere, and she would drag all of us along..."

His words sounded happy, and looking at his face, I would have thought that he was enjoying these memories. But underneath there was a layer of sadness, as if he were aware that every step he took brought him one little bit closer to the end of everything. *This is the last time I will take this walk*, he thought. *And I won't see Nicole this year when she comes home for Christmas.*

What if I can't save him? I thought. *What if he ends up like every other soul in that Abyss, screaming out for reprieve, when there is none to be found?* I didn't want to believe it, but as I listened to the train of his thoughts, I couldn't help but think his damnation was inevitable.

"Carrie, are you all right?" Sebastian stopped walking and grabbed my arm to stop me, too. "You're crying."

I lifted my hand to my face and realized that was true.

"You told me you would tell me if your feet hurt too badly! Come on. Let's sit down."

It seemed easier to let him guide me to sit by the creek than to explain that my tears had nothing to do with any physical pain. "Thank you. I'll be all right in a minute."

He stared into the water. "This is where it happened, you know. I mean not this exact spot, but here in the park. I was walking along here, thinking about Felicity, and I wanted to save her more than anything. I was so angry with God right then, for taking her away, and I guess that anger left a gap for a demon to sneak in."

"You think there was something about you that brought her here." I could feel the emotions hovering under the surface of his mind. "You think you must have somehow been damned already if it meant a demon could reach you. It's not true; that's not how it works. The archdemons prefer to gather good souls when they can, especially Azrael. She chooses people who will do anything for someone they love; she hates God so much for casting her out that she uses His greatest gift as a weapon to hurt him. It wasn't your anger that called Azrael to you; it was your love."

He gave me a small smile. "Somehow, that doesn't make me feel that much better. Maybe Felicity is right; maybe I should have trusted that God knew what He was doing in taking her away and not interfered. She says it was my pride talking, thinking that I could somehow improve upon God's plan. I don't think that was it, though. I didn't want to have to live in a world where that plan involved my sister's death."

"It wasn't pride. If it had been pride, Lucifer would have come for you, himself." Though I suspected that Lucifer was sorry that he missed out on collecting Sebastian's soul. He always liked to be directly involved in the major contracts, and the damnation of a righteous soul was surely unique enough for his tastes.

He looked back out at the water. "I wish there were another way. I mean, I'm not sorry I did it, really. I know that Felicity is going to do great things with her life, greater than I would have done. And I believe that one day, there will be a final reckoning between God and Satan that will free all the souls in Hell, so it's not like I will be there forever. But I still wish there could have been another way to save her."

I wanted to tell him that he was right, but after spending four nights listening to the souls in Hell, I doubted that Sebastian would maintain his sanity long enough to appreciate freedom. If God ever bothered to grant it, and I was far from certain that would ever happen.

We sat in silence for a few minutes, both of our thoughts spiraling further downward, but soon he forced a smile onto his face. "We should get going. Still things to do!"

"Where to next?" I asked as we walked along Chestnut Street. Other people seemed to have the same idea that we had and were out enjoying the June evening.

"I have reservations at Morimoto," Sebastian said.

I slowed as we passed the Philadelphia History Museum, glancing at their list of exhibits. "I've wanted to eat there, but Bedlam never likes to eat anywhere you need reservations more than a few days in advance."

Sebastian had gotten ahead of me, so I hurried to catch up.

"Is he, like, your boyfriend or something?" he asked.

"Or something." I never liked trying to explain Bedlam's and my relationship to anyone. How did you tell a mortal what it was like to have only one friend for three thousand years? "Anyway, you must have made these reservations months ago."

We passed by a small Indian restaurant, and the scent of spicy curry filled the air. "Well, I've known for a while when the end was coming. I planned to drag Felicity with me, but she hates Asian food."

I glanced sideways at him. "Somehow, I think she'd make an exception."

He stopped suddenly to avoid a woman stepping out of a nail salon. "Probably, but it's more fun to go with someone who actually enjoys it."

I guess. "If she hates Asian food, she must have had a hard time in Japan these past few months, then."

Sebastian laughed. "That she did." He turned to look at me. "Wait. How did you know about that?"

"She met my friend Gabriel there. He's the one who told her where to find me." I considered how to best describe

Gabriel to Sebastian. "He's the only angel I've ever met who would actually get his hands dirty cleaning up after a storm."

"Well, it's nice there's one out there, I guess." We reached Morimoto, and he pulled the door open, gesturing that I should go inside.

We ordered the *omakase*, and Sebastian insisted on paying. I'm not exactly sure what the first course was, and the miso soup tasted a little bland, but that was followed by some outstanding fish from the raw bar. We cleansed our palettes with some Asian fusion sorbet made of some fruit that I had never heard of and then moved on to the heart of the meal. We tried a delicious snapper served in some citrus sauce, followed by crispy duck and a selection of assorted sushi. By dessert, we were both full, but we managed to make room for the chocolate cake and hazelnut mousse.

Our next stop was an ordinary bar, crowded, most of the tables full of people huddled over small pieces of paper. A man wearing the bar's T-shirt stood at the front of the room, adjusting a microphone. "It's quizzo night," Sebastian said. "Bar trivia."

I must have looked puzzled.

"They ask questions, and the team that gets the most right wins a free tab for the night. I used to play all the time in college."

I looked around the room. The teams seemed to be made up of four or five people. "Are you sure we can do it on our own?"

Sebastian frowned. "Well, usually I have a bigger team, but it doesn't matter if we win."

"I suppose."

As I moved toward one of the few free tables in the bar, I picked up a random thought: *Damn it, Stephanie and*

Greg aren't coming. Now we're down two more players. I turned to see who thought that, and I found two college-aged girls, a blond and a brunette, sitting at a half-empty table. I pointed them out to Sebastian and moved in that direction.

"Hi, I'm Carrie, and this is Sebastian. We're in desperate need of a team, and we were wondering if you needed some more people."

"Definitely." The blond moved her purse off the chair to her right so that I could sit next to her. "We're lucky you came along. I'm Greta."

"I'm Marilyn." The other girl reached out to shake our hands. "I hope one of you knows something about history, because we hate losing."

We made a pretty good team, we discovered as the night went on. Marilyn had four brothers and consequently knew a great deal about sports, which was useful because I never would have remembered that Jacques Anquetil won the Tour de France four years in a row in the 1960s. Greta was a biology major who could answer things entirely beyond my knowledge, like what HNO_3 was and where the superior vena cava was located, though I suppose I should have learned that on my many trips through the heart that morning. Sebastian had spent a summer volunteering in Nigeria, so he knew that it had the largest population in Africa. And as for me, I can only say that a lot of the questions seemed less obscure when you had actually lived through the events.

At the end of the night, we were tied with one of the other teams. I had drunk some sake back at the restaurant and was on my third beer at the bar, which was more alcohol than I was accustomed to consuming, so I actually laughed aloud when the tiebreaker question was "What was the name of the river in the Ancient Greek Underworld that allowed its drinker to forget?"

"I don't know, but I think she threw me across the room

last night." Bedlam would have laughed, but my audience had no idea what I was talking about. They were grateful, though, that my personal knowledge of the demon of mercy won us a free bar tab for the night.

We finished our drinks and chatted with Greta and Marilyn for a little bit, but Sebastian's heart wasn't in it. *This is it,* he thought. *No more quizzo. No more last day. No more anything.* At the earliest polite break in conversation, I asked Sebastian, who had stuck to drinking soda, to drive me back to the diner.

"Thanks for inviting me out today. I had a lot of fun. I had kind of forgotten what it was like to be out with people." I pulled on the door handle and let myself out.

He forced a smile. "I had a good time, too. I'd invite you out again, but my schedule is pretty packed for the foreseeable future."

I tried to force a smile to match his, but I found I couldn't quite manage it. "I'm sorry." I planned to do what I could to save him, but in case I failed, I wanted him to know how I felt about it. "I'm sorry I couldn't do more to help you."

He leaned over and kissed my cheek. "You did help, Carrie. You made it so I didn't have to go through this alone, and that means everything to me." *Should I ask her? No, it would be too much.*

"What is it?"

He smiled, but it didn't reach his eyes. "Can't keep anything from you, can I? I just wanted to ask... Would you be there? You know, when she comes for me, could you be there with me?"

"Of course." If I failed to save him, I at least owed him not having to face his death alone. "Let me know when and where."

He wrote down an address and told me to be there before eight p.m. on Saturday. I promised him that I would.

CHAPTER 15

THAT NIGHT, MY JOURNEY TO Hell started out like the others. I selected one of the three remaining focal points and started toward it. I was running out of time to save Sebastian, and I was more desperate to do so than ever. Since I had spent the day with him, he wasn't just a person who was being forced by a disinterested God to fulfill an unjust contract. He was also a man with a life and a family and a sense of humor and a plethora of absurd pieces of trivia regarding African demographics.

When I fully coalesced in the Hellscape, I was standing on the lawn I had seen at a distance from Lilith's woods, which flickered between to the approach to my cave in Greece and the entrance to my Paris apartment. There were a limited number of archdemons left for me to encounter, and I had a sinking suspicion of whose domain I had stumbled into—a suspicion that was confirmed when I heard a series of loud snarling noises coming from behind me.

I turned and saw a two large gleaming yellow eyes staring back at me. I flicked my gaze to the side and could make out the forms of several crouching wild animals.

A flash of lightning lit up the sky, and for one instant I beheld the hulking black bulldog known as the Beast. The only demon who had an animal form instead of a human one hunkered down and growled, signaling to his pack of Hellhounds that they could attack at will.

Run! The souls of the damned seemed to egg the dogs on as they started toward me.

I glanced from side to side. No door, not that I expected one. Mephistopheles said the Beast would seek payment in blood, and I didn't expect to see an exit until I had paid my due.

I turned and ran. I didn't know where I was going, but instinct drove me to put as much distance as possible between me and the slobbering hounds. I looked up—there was a door right in front of me, the entrance to the house. Perhaps the Beast offered the same deal as Lilith: If I could get to the door before his minions attacked, I would earn my freedom.

Closer.

I sprinted toward the worn wooden porch, but the pack snapped at my heels. I could never outrun them. My only hope was to get close enough to the door that I could pull myself through after the attack was done, if the demon dogs didn't drag me back to their lair.

I stepped up onto the first stair. Before I could proceed to the next, sharp teeth dug into my leg. The mouth holding me yanked me backwards, and I lost my balance. I fell, catching myself on the stairs with my hands.

Feed.

One after the other, a dozen or so Hellhounds descended on me where I lay. Sharp teeth dug into my calf, ripping away flesh. I screamed in agony as sharp claws mauled my stomach. Incisors gripped my ankle and dragged me backward. I cried out as I bumped down the wooden stairs, splinters digging into my open wounds. I rolled into a fetal position.

I sobbed through the blows until I felt as though the dogs had torn open all the skin on my legs, arms, and back. My clothes lay shredded around me. I heard a loud bark, and the hounds backed away from me, gnashing their teeth. Thinking that they were done with the attack, I moved my shaking hands away from my face, hoping to see an opening through which I could escape.

No mercy.

Instead, I beheld the face of the massive black bulldog who led the pack. My entire body quivered with fear at the sight of his drooling mouth and mammoth incisors. Yet I couldn't look away when he lifted one large paw above my head and swiped my face with his razor-sharp claws.

The force of the hit knocked my head against the ground, and I passed out.

CHAPTER 16

I DRIFTED IN AND OUT OF consciousness as I lay on the lawn of the Hell mansion. Some part of me knew that I needed to get up and get out of there, but that part was overruled by the part that was in excruciating pain and wanted to be unconscious. But I couldn't stay here forever. Who knew what the Beast would do, if he came back and I was still in his realm?

I rolled onto my stomach, gasping as I stretched my wounded abdomen. I didn't remember getting those gashes. The Beast must have kept attacking me even after I passed out.

I pushed myself onto my hands and knees, gritting my teeth as dirt ground into my wounds. I pulled myself forward a few agonizing inches at a time. *You've been hurt worse,* I told myself, even though I wasn't sure it was true. But if I made it back to my body, I would heal eventually. Part of my immortality was the ability to completely heal from any injury that was not caused by an angelic sword.

At last I reached the stairs. I lay my head down on the stoop, cringing as the splinters in the wood brushed against the open wounds on my cheek.

I closed my eyes. *I'll just rest here a minute.*

I awoke to hear someone yelling. "I need you to come back now. Please, Khet!"

Bedlam, and he sounded fairly desperate. I hoped he

hadn't come down to Hell with me. Lucifer would be sure to find and imprison him. I thought that I should probably get up and check because I didn't want him to be stuck in Hell forever. He deserved better than that.

I lifted one knee onto the bottom step, then cringed at the pressure as I raised the other knee to match it. I repeated the arduous process twice more, trying not to notice the trail of blood I left behind on the stairs. At last my whole body lay on the porch. I tried to see where Bedlam was, but one of my eyes was swollen shut, and my neck hurt too much to turn my head.

I listened instead, but I couldn't hear anything. He was gone, or maybe he was never there in the first place. Much as I would like to think that a grievous injury on my part would send Bedlam into a hysterical panic, I knew it wouldn't. He was incapable of remembering my existence when he had Keziel on the brain.

And then, as if to prove the power of my suggestive mind, I felt Keziel's presence. Because even in my own delirious fantasies, I couldn't think of Bedlam without her intruding. "Why did you do this to yourself, Cassia? You know you shouldn't upset Bedlam like that."

Me, upset him? I wanted to scream back at her. *I don't upset him. You're the one who upsets him, you crazy bitch!*

My anger motivated me to scrape my raw legs a few inches closer to the door, but then the effort made me collapse again. If I stretched my hand out a bit more, I could touch the frame, but I didn't have the energy even for that, and I passed out again.

"Cassia?" I woke up to hear my name whispered hesitantly by a male voice. "Cassia, can you hear me?"

Gabriel? I reached out with my mind to see if the angel was nearby, but I couldn't feel his presence. I could just hear his voice coming from the other side of the door.

It didn't sound quite like him, but who else would call me Cassia?

"Cassia, if you can hear me, it's time to come back now. Just follow my voice." He sounded so concerned and not at all accusatory, not the faintest hint of *I told you so*. I wondered again if it were a figment of my imagination, but if there was a chance that Gabriel had come back and had forgiven me, even though I ended up in exactly the situation he had warned me against, I owed it to him to go back.

I forced myself up on my knees and reached for the door handle. It took me a few tries to grasp it firmly enough to turn it, and I had to gather all my strength to push it open. From there, though, it was just a matter of falling with enough of my mass over the threshold to get out of Hell.

I opened my eyes back in my bedroom. Well, I opened one of my eyes, since the other one—along with half of my face—appeared to be covered in some kind of bandage. I felt a presence next to me, one that reminded me of Gabriel but weaker. I turned my head a slight amount to see if my angel had really come back to me, but I found even that small motion was too much for me.

"Bedlam!" The voice was pitched too low to be Gabriel's. "She's awake."

The demon almost immediately appeared in my line of sight. "Khet!" His eyes widened with relief. "Thank God! Are you okay?"

I tried to answer but found that I couldn't speak, with the several layers of gauze covering my mouth. I settled for trying to make my uncovered eye seem as reassuring as possible, though I suspected that the fact that I required so much bandaging detracted from the overall message. I then tried to glance to the side in a questioning manner, asking who was sitting next to me.

"Oh, it's Sebastian." He pulled the young man whose soul I had still not saved into my line of vision. "See?"

"Hi, Carrie." Sebastian was worried about me as well. "Are you all right? What happened?"

I tried to communicate to him that I was fine, but he was not as adept as Bedlam at reading complex sentiments from only a quarter of my face. "Lilith's bow, she can't talk right now," the demon said. "And you need to go before your sister sends out a barrage of Jesuits for me or something." He turned back to me to explain. "I needed to get Sebastian to come help you, and his sister seemed to think I was the evil kind of demon that she couldn't trust. Crazy, right?"

I arched my eyebrow at him, and he laughed.

I can't believe he's laughing when she's hurt like that. The legs of the chair Sebastian sat on squeaked as he stood up. "I need to go now, but I'll come back and check on you tomorrow, okay, Carrie?"

I raised my hand in the closest approximation I could make to a wave farewell and tried not to wish that he had been Gabriel instead.

"Did you think he was Gabriel?" I was surprised Bedlam had caught wind of the direction of my thoughts. "That was the plan. I didn't know how else to get you back. You didn't seem to hear me."

I did hear you, I tried to tell him, but he wrinkled his nose at me. Maybe he was right. Maybe I hadn't heard him. I thought I had heard Keziel too, and I couldn't imagine her being here to help me out.

"Good news is, Keziel bandaged your wounds, so you should heal quickly. She has all that mother nature healing power stuff, so you should be back to normal in no time." I felt the bandage tape rip as my brow furrowed in concern, but Bedlam responded to me before he saw my face. "Stop worrying about me. You should see yourself. I get to do all the worrying, right now."

He returned to my line of vision, holding a glass of water in one hand and a pile of books in the other hand. "Hey, you didn't tell Michael about Kezi coming here, did you? She came by all upset because someone tattled." I gave him my very best *When have I ever sought out Michael over anything?* look, and he laughed. "That's what I said. But apparently someone told him. Must have been Gabs." He shrugged and forgot about it.

What about the diner? This was the third time this week I had slept through opening time. Dwayne and Madame Zarita would think I had become unreliable.

"Don't worry about the diner," Bedlam said, once again seeming to read my mind. "It's closed. I sent Dwayne and Madame Zarita home and told them we'd call them when you were feeling better. They were more concerned than anything."

He held the glass out to me. "Okay, I have some water if you're thirsty..." He trailed off, eying the bandages covering my mouth. "Um. I guess we can take those off if you really want some." I shook my head in as large a 'no' as I could manage, and he set the cup on my nightstand and held out the books. "I can also read to you if you want. I have your very favorite books. Whatever you want, Khet."

Curious as I was to find out what Bedlam thought my very favorite books were, I wanted to sleep more than anything else. I closed my eye for several seconds to convey that.

"Yeah, sleep is probably the best thing for you right now. I will stay right here the whole time, so you don't have to worry about anything."

I opened my hand slightly, and he reached out and took it. *Thank you. I love you.*

He ran his other hand along my hair above where my forehead was showing. "It's you and me, Khet. Forever and ever and always. You know that."

I smiled at him, even though he couldn't see it, and drifted off to sleep.

"Are you done eating?" Bedlam asked me on Friday night, two days later.

By then, most of the bandages had come off my face—thanks, no doubt, to Keziel, even though I had no desire to be in her debt. Maybe I could get her a fruit basket and call it a day. I was able to sit up in bed and eat off a tray that he had procured from somewhere.

"Just about." I picked up the last bit of garlic bread and put it in my mouth. "Though I'm still a little concerned that you made an entire meal without adding any of your creative ingredients." He had made me *al dente* spaghetti with a lightly seasoned meat sauce, complete with the bread and a side salad with Italian dressing. "At least tell me that my kitchen is a disaster area, so I don't think that you've been possessed by an angel or something."

He stuck out his tongue at me as he picked up the tray. "You got ripped up by the most vicious demon in Hell. I'm allowed to be worried about you for a few days. Let me take this downstairs, and then we can find out if Emma and Frank Churchill are really meant for each other. Just between you and me, I think he might turn out to be a cad."

Now it was my turn to stick my tongue out at him. "We don't have to read Jane Austen if you don't want to."

Bedlam shrugged. "It's not that I mind reading *Emma* for the nine millionth time. I just think the story would be improved if Jane Fairfax had lasers or something."

I shook my head and was about to tell him that he had no appreciation for fine literature when someone else stuck his head up into my apartment. "Sebastian! You shouldn't be here. You should be spending time with your family." He had come to visit me Thursday as well, and I had said the same thing then.

He set his jaw and entered the room. "It's my last few

days on earth. I can spend them doing whatever I want."

Bedlam moved past him to leave the room with the tray. "Looks like this is going to be a fun visit. I'll be downstairs cleaning up, if anyone needs me."

I watched his back as he descended down the stairs. "I'm trying not to worry about what the kitchen looks like right now." I glanced back at Sebastian, who was sitting in the chair next to my bed. "And he must be leaving the door unlocked, if you got in, so everything in the kitchen might get stolen before I get down there."

"He seems to be taking good care of you, though."

I turned my head back to Sebastian. "Oh, he's been perfect. He's even letting me use the good pillow. Between that and the fact that he's covered up the mirror in the bathroom, I can only assume I look absolutely terrible."

Sebastian frowned. "Well, I don't think the 'mauled by a wild animal' look is going to be hitting the pages of any of my sister's favorite fashion magazines this season. But considering how you looked a few days ago, I would say you're doing pretty well. Can I assume you still aren't going to tell me what happened?"

"Oh, it was stupid. I was walking in the woods and not paying attention. I forget that being immortal doesn't mean I can't get seriously hurt." I made myself smile. "But I've been bored, sitting here for two days. What have you been up to?"

Am I actually supposed to believe that story? Though I can't think what else could have happened to make her look like that. I guess it doesn't matter, because she's not going to tell me what's really going on, anyway. "Oh, not much. Hanging out with my family. My dad is giving me grief about not going to law school. I told him I'd apply next year, since it's easier than explaining why I won't be around." He picked up a few of the books sitting in a pile next to my bed and started flipping through them. "So you're a big Austen fan?"

I glanced at the covers of the books he held up. "I don't have much space for books in this apartment, so I only keep a few around. I confess to being a huge fan of the girly classics. Jane Austen, Elizabeth Gaskell, *Wuthering Heights*."

"No *Jane Eyre*?"

"I hate *Jane Eyre*. It never made any sense to me that people of such differing social classes would fall in love." And I wasn't projecting too much or anything. "I'd go to the library, but they revoked my card after Bedlam lost a few too many best-sellers. And I'm not sure that I trust him to pick stuff out, anyway."

"That is unfair. My taste is unquestioned." Bedlam appeared at the top of the stairs, leaning on the doorframe.

"Mmm-hmm. And whose idea was it to read those books with the glittering dead people and the girl who couldn't decide between the zombie and the collie?"

"That's not quite... did you hit your head too?" Bedlam looked at Sebastian. "What are the signs of a concussion?"

"I think she's messing with you." Sebastian looked between the two of us and then stood up. "Much as I would love to stay here and discuss the great literary works of our day, I must confess that I need to go meet my family for dinner."

"Thanks for stopping by," I said.

Sebastian leaned forward and kissed my cheek. "No problem. I'll come back tomorrow if I can, and I'll try to bring you a new book. If not..." He didn't need to finish the sentence. We both knew where he would be after tomorrow.

Bedlam watched him go and then turned back to me with my eyes narrowed. "Don't even think it."

"Don't even think what?"

He walked over and sat down in the chair that Sebastian had vacated. "Don't even think about trying to save his soul again. It's too late, Khet, and he made his choice."

"But Bedlam..."

He set his mouth in a firm line. "I never should have let you go in the first place. If I had been paying the proper amount of attention, I would have stopped you."

I sank down lower in my bed. "It wasn't supposed to go on so long. The goal was to find Azrael and get out. It was just bad luck that she wasn't one of the first five places I tried."

He leaned forward, narrowing his eyes. "Bad luck? Bad luck does not lead to your having to confront five archdemons in as many days. You need a dose of pure idiocy to do that. And don't tell me you did it for Sebastian, because there is no way that he would even think to ask you to do this for him."

I turned away from him and started fiddling with one of the pillows. "I'm not doing it just for him. I'm doing it because it's right, because I refuse to live in a universe that allows good people to go to Hell if I can stop it."

"Well, you can't stop it, because I absolutely forbid you to return to Hell."

I rolled my eyes and looked back at him. "Like you could actually stop me if I decided to go. You can't physically restrain my spirit, Bedlam."

He wrinkled his face. *She's right, damn it, but there has to be something I can do. Ooh I know!* "I can't stop you, but I can follow you if you leave. If you go to Hell, I'm going with you."

He had me there, and he knew it. If he went down into Hell, either Lucifer or Beelzebub was sure to restrain him and cast him out into the Abyss. And now that I had seen the Abyss, I understood why he had spent more than three thousand years avoiding that punishment.

I'll have to figure out some way to go without him finding out.

He picked up *Emma* and continued reading to me for a little while, but after a few chapters I yawned, feigning sleepiness.

"No, no, no." Bedlam put down the book and leaned over. "You can't go to sleep yet. It's way too early, and I will be bored."

"I apologize if my desire to sleep offends you." I yawned again for effect. "Some of us are still recovering from a Hellhound attack."

Bedlam leaned back and crossed his arms. "Well, now what am I supposed to do? I'm not tired at all."

As far as I could tell, he shouldn't have ever been tired. He rematerialized refreshed every time he teleported, which he did multiple times a day. But I had never seen much logic in what Bedlam could and could not do with his powers, and I didn't want to argue about it.

"Well, you have declared that if you have to read *Wives and Daughters* one more time, your head will explode. While I would love to prove you wrong on that count, you could go get something new for us to read tomorrow."

Ooh, good idea! Except I really shouldn't leave her alone in case she starts bleeding again or something. "Are you sure you'll be okay?"

"There's a Barnes & Noble at Rittenhouse Square you can go to and be back before I've even noticed you're gone." I worried he might even be gone too short a time, but I counted on him getting distracted.

Bedlam considered. "Well, I'll only be gone a little while. And you'll be asleep the whole time?" I assured him that I would, grateful that he did not have the power to detect lies. So he left, and I thanked a disinterested God that Bedlam was capricious enough to have let his boredom distract him from being suspicious of me.

With another two prayers to that same God, one to forgive me for deceiving my friend and one that the fifty percent chance that I had to find Azrael would work in my favor, I closed my eyes and prepared to go to Hell.

CHAPTER 17

I APPROACHED ONE OF THE LAST two centers of power in Hell, and once again I found myself in the candlelit hallway that looked out onto the bleak moor.

After I passed through a doorway, I found myself in a bedroom with red-papered walls and black wood furniture, carved to match Mephistopheles's and Beelzebub's. My surroundings flickered intermittently to my Spartan bedroom in the temple to Isis and my current apartment in Philadelphia, which by some strange chance had the same color curtains as the one I was in, though the ones there were thick velvet, trimmed with thick black cords.

Demons of both genders stood throughout the room, looking like jaded models on the set of some S&M advertisement. The garish makeup on their bored faces looked even more macabre in the flickering candlelight than they would have in normal lighting. The female succubi wore corsets made of wire and red lace, and their stockings were held up by black leather garters. The male incubi wore black leather harnesses that left little to the imagination.

In one corner, twin brunette succubae had a blond incubus chained to the wall with wrought iron. They took turns hitting him with sharp-tipped whips that left thin strips of blood across his bare alabaster chest. Next to them, one demon appeared to be choking another, who seemed on the verge of passing out. A brief glance at the trio to their right was enough for me to know that I didn't want to see more of what they were doing, at least until they put some more clothes on.

A nearby demon's eyes flicked over me in disdain, and I glanced down at myself. I had a tomato stain on my wrinkled white T-shirt, and there was a hole in the left knee of my blue sweatpants. My green socks had monkeys stitched onto them and were almost worn through at the toes. The numerous Band-Aids on my arms covered the scratches there, but they only reminded me that my face looked far worse. And, of course, I hadn't brushed my hair in about three days.

But I refused to let a demon look down on me, so I met the eye of each incubus or succubus. In every case, it was the demon who broke eye contact.

Never good enough, the souls whispered in my head.

"Who's there?" At the sound of the sultry female voice, the incubi and succubi sashayed aside so that I was in full view of the king-sized bed in the center of the room. The black wooden posts were topped with a red velvet canopy trimmed in black lace, and the crimson covers on the bed were made of silk and satin. Lounging on the bed, amidst a pile of plush pillows and fawning demons, lay a red-haired beauty dressed in a more elaborate version of the succubae's garb.

The archdemon Azrael smiled, but her black eyes remained hard and cold. "Well, well, well. The little Oracle has finally come to see me."

I stepped forward, meeting her eyes. "You talked to Mephistopheles, then?"

"Indeed. You see, Mephistopheles and I have something of an arrangement. He claims to be all about the cerebral realm, but when it comes right down to it, men are all the same." She was trying to shock me by implying illicit relations between herself and Mephistopheles. Sex without love was forbidden among angels, but I was a human, so it took more than that to scandalize me. "I had rather expected to see you sooner, though. It's been over a week since I heard you were looking for me."

Too late.

The velvet hanging down from the canopy looked so soft that I couldn't help running my fingers over it. "I didn't mean to keep you waiting. I was somewhat distracted by some of your compatriots."

"I can see that." She eyed my injuries. "Of course, I suspect that each of my fellows took their tolls in other, less visible ways. I have wanted to meet you for some time now, Cama. It is Cama, isn't it? That's what Mephistopheles says, though I have heard other names. Callidora, Corinna, Khet. I do wonder which you prefer."

No one.

I looked at her and found myself drawn in by the beauty of her features: the slant of her black eyes, the lush red of her lips, the curve of her white neck. "It makes no difference to me what you call me. I go by Carrie now, if that's what you wish to use."

"Carrie, hmm? Ordinary and uninspiring." She pouted for a moment, but then her lips again turned up in a smile. "I find that, overall, seeing you is rather exciting. After all, it is not every day that one meets a human with the audacity to love an angel."

I must have looked surprised, because she chuckled.

"Oh, yes, little Carrie. That is my special gift, you see. I can look at anyone and tell who they love. Keziel, Lilith, and the like—they can hide their feelings from themselves, but they cannot hide them from me. I wonder if you are like them. Do you need me to tell you who holds your affections?"

No love.

I pulled my gaze from her lips and forced myself to meet her eyes. "I think I know my own heart."

"You probably do." She pouted at my refusal to take her bait. "Now, then, I believe you sought me out for a purpose, did you not?"

"I did." I took a deep breath. My heart beat fast, and my hands shook. "You laid claim to the soul of one Sebastian Connolly." Much to my surprise, I managed to keep my voice steady. "I would like you to void your contract and relinquish that claim."

She stood up and stretched, and my eyes couldn't help but follow her cat-like movements. "Now, I obtained that soul fair and square. Why should I release it?"

No escape.

"Because he doesn't belong here!" Such an argument would mean nothing to one such as Azrael, but I had to at least try to make it. "Because he is a good and uncorrupted person, who is willing to give up everything for someone he loves, and he doesn't deserve to be trapped here forever."

Azrael looked Heavenward, as if asking for strength from a divine source, then slunk over to the demon being whipped in the corner. "Darling, all those things make him *more* valuable to me, and me less inclined to let him go. I mean, imagine it! How impressed everyone would be! Not even Lucifer has a good soul in his possession."

Only evil.

"What do you want in exchange?" There had to be something she wanted, or she wouldn't have been having that discussion with me.

"Let me see." She took a whip from one of the girls and waved both of them away. "For me to give up Sebastian, I would need to have something of even greater value. Another soul, I think, for nothing else can have quite so much value. But what soul could be worth more than that of a good man? I can only think of one, and that would be..." She paused, and her smile broadened as she met my eyes. "... yours."

Join us.

My mouth dropped open. I hadn't given much thought to what she would ask for—because, as she said, there wasn't much that would have more value to a demon than a good soul. But I thought that even Azrael would be smarter than to try to claim mine. "But I can't die."

She snapped her whip against the chained man's chest. "Who said that you had to die in order to give me your soul? You're here now, aren't you?" Clearly she had given this offer a lot of thought. "If I were to force you to stay down here, Lucifer would intervene, but God still has more power than any demon, though He seldom chooses to exercise it. He gave all humans—even aberrant ones like you—the gift that He denied His angels: free will. So if you agree to come with me of your own volition, your body will still technically be alive, and Lucifer cannot stand against it."

Powerless.

Azrael knelt down in front of her victim as I considered her logic. I was not certain that things would play out as she described. I did know that if she was right, she was playing a dangerous game, humiliating Lucifer. But, then, she had never chosen to serve under him as the other demons had, and she had likely been seeking a way to spite him since the Fall.

She leaned forward and inhaled over the place where the incubus bled. Her eyes rolled back in her head, as if the scent of blood were intoxicating. These were hardly the environs in which I wanted to spend eternity. But I had to ask myself, if it were up to me, was my soul a price I was willing to pay? I found I didn't even need to consider the answer. My long life could at last be over, and Sebastian could go off to law school and become a public defender and find a nice girl to marry and live a real, full life. I couldn't say I looked forward to an eternity in the Abyss, but I hadn't enjoyed my immortality, either. And maybe when my body was an all-but-lifeless husk, Lucifer would realize that he couldn't hold up his end of the bargain and would free the souls that had been exchanged for my eternal life.

Azrael stuck out her long tongue and licked the blood from the gash on her minion's chest. And even as her actions disgusted me, I knew. One good soul and maybe ten more in exchange for my one? It was not even a contest.

Forever with us.

I made sure to keep my expression neutral. "I might consider it. Would I have the traditional three years left on earth?"

She laughed, and all her demons joined in her amusement. "Don't be absurd. You would be taking over Sebastian's contract, so I would come for you at his appointed time."

So tomorrow night, then. "But you will let me leave here and go back to earth until that time comes?" I wanted to make sure I at least got a chance to say good-bye to Bedlam and to try to explain. To Gabriel, too, if I could find him.

"Oh, why not?" Azrael sauntered over to me waving her whip, motions that managed to be both sexy and menacing. I gulped as she leaned toward me, frightened that she was going to strike me with it. She turned and wrapped it around the neck of an incubus to my right.

I hoped she didn't notice my sigh of relief. "And as long as I agree, Sebastian goes free? You will remove your sigil from him immediately? And as long as I am willing to go with you at the appointed time, he gets what he asked for? His sister gets to live?"

"Yes, yes, of course. You agree, and I will never come near the boy or his family again. They can live their long, happy, boring human lives. Do we have an agreement or not?"

I swallowed and took a deep breath, then nodded. "We do."

She laughed and snapped the whip off the demon, leaving a bleeding ring around his throat. At the same time, the back of my hand began to burn. I looked down and found that I had Azrael's sigil etched into my skin. I assumed the identical mark on Sebastian's hand had been removed.

Azrael smirked at me. "I'll see you tomorrow, Carrie." She gestured behind me, and I saw that a door out of the bedroom had appeared.

I nodded with as much dignity as I could muster and left Hell for the last time.

CHAPTER 18

BEDLAM HADN'T RETURNED WHEN I got back. *Probably just as well,* I thought, but I wanted him to return soon so that I could get the process of telling him what happened over with.

After what felt like an eternity, he materialized in my room holding a larger bag than I would have thought his quest warranted. "Okay, so I didn't know what to get so I..." He stopped and stared at me. "What did you do?"

He teleported to sit directly in front of me. He grabbed my shoulders as the bag he had left behind fell to the floor with a clatter. "*What did you do?*"

I flinched back, hiding my hand behind my back. I didn't think I had ever seen him this angry—at least, not directed at me. "I had to."

He jumped up on his feet and paced around the room. After a moment, he faced me. "No, you did not *have* to! There is no way that anyone could conceive that you *had* to sell your soul to a demon, not for any reason! Sebastian didn't want you to do it for him, and I'm pretty sure he would make you take it back if he did find out!"

"It wasn't just for him, Bedlam." I was surprised to find that my voice was steady, and no tears formed in my eyes. "If I go to Hell, I'll be all but dead, and maybe Lucifer will let the souls that died for me go."

Bedlam made an exasperated noise. "That wasn't your fault either, Khet!" He held up his hand to stop me from interrupting. "I know, I know. The universe holds you responsible for it, or something like that. Who cares what the universe thinks? The universe thinks that I'm supposed to be in Hell too, and you're the one who keeps telling me that it's me who decides my place, not anybody else. Are you telling me that's not true? Because let me tell you, Khet, if you belong in Hell, then I sure as suffering do, too."

Tears started to well up. "Oh, Bedlam, no. That's not true at all. I'm just... different from you. You're an angel; you were meant to live forever, and for you, there is always hope. For me, there is nothing but the knowledge that I will remain here, and the people I love will continue to suffer for it. This way, maybe they will be free."

He gaped at me. "Hope for me? Khet, there isn't any hope for me. Nothing short of a miracle could send me back to Heaven, and I'm not even sure I want that. What would I do up there? Follow Michael's orders? Pretend it doesn't kill me to see Kezi and Jophi together every single day? I belong in Heaven even less than I belong in Hell. The only person that I feel like I belong with is you, and you're going to be gone. Where's the hope in that?"

I'm going to be alone again, he thought. *I can't do it. I can't go back to that.*

I gasped at the emptiness of this vision in his head. "I'm sorry. I didn't know." The first tear rolled down my cheek.

He whipped his head around to face me, eyes narrowed. "You didn't know what? You know everything."

The tears fell faster. "I don't. Sometimes, when I feel something, I can't tell if it's me or somebody else feeling it. I didn't know you needed me as badly as I need you."

He knelt next to the bed and looked up at me, his black eyes begging me to reconsider my deal. "But I do need you, Khet. So, please, take it back."

I wanted to tell him that I would if I could, but even though it devastated him, I couldn't say I was sorry I made the deal. "I can't. Azrael thinks she traded up for my soul. She won't accept a reversal now."

193

Bedlam sat down on his feet, deflated.

"Hey." I reached out my hand to him. "I have one more day. Let's pretend that it's a normal night and do whatever we would ordinarily do. Like, you can show me what you bought."

"All right." *As if I'm going to forget she's abandoning me.* "I wasn't sure what kind of books you would want. So I got you one of those e-book readers. I thought it would save you from having to go out again while you were recovering." His voice thickened on the last words, as he realized that I would not be getting any better.

"That was really thoughtful of you." I reached out to take it from him. "Show me how it works."

We spent longer figuring out how to get the device functioning than most people would have, since we gave new meaning to the concept of being too old to adapt to new technology. Once we finally got it working, Bedlam spent the rest of the night reading to me. I grew drowsy as the night went on, but these were my last few hours to spend with the people I loved, and I wasn't going to waste them sleeping.

When the first rays of morning sun peeked through my window, I stretched, then cringed as the movement pulled at the gash on my abdomen. "I'm opening the diner today."

Bedlam didn't look up from the Terry Pratchett book in front of him. (His choice, not mine.) "No, you're not. You still look like you got half your face clawed off, and you can barely stand. Besides, why would you want to spend your last day on earth slaving away at the worst eatery in the city?"

"Because I want Dwayne to have at least one more day of income." I moved to stand up, but Bedlam was on the side of the bed that wasn't against the wall. I pushed at him to make him get up and tried to ignore what the pressure did to the scrape on my arm.

He refused to move. "He hasn't seemed that upset at having no work the past couple of days."

I pushed the blankets back and crawled around him. He tried to block me with his legs, but he didn't want to hit any of my bruises too hard, so I was able to push past him. "I want a normal day, Bedlam. The diner is normal."

Bedlam watched me limp over to my closet. "That would be much more convincing if you could actually stand up straight."

I pulled a loose blue dress off the hanger and turned around to get the rest of my clothes out of the dresser. "You're not changing my mind."

Bedlam sighed. "Fine. But I'm waiting on all the tables."

I laughed as I walked back across the room, moving as quickly as I could, when every step sent bursts of pain up my leg. "You're doing work? This I've got to see."

I had Bedlam call Dwayne to tell him to come in while I took a shower. The water soothed my aching muscles, so I stayed longer than was necessary. As I was toweling my hair dry, I stuck my head out of the door. "Do me a favor?"

"Depends what it is."

I rolled my eyes. "Can you go over and check on Sebastian? I want to make sure Azrael removed his mark."

Bedlam stretched and resumed reading. "Yeah, sure. I'll go as soon as I make sure you're not going to fall down the stairs."

"I am perfectly capable of walking!" I hung the towel on the hook on the back of the door and marched to the stairs. I might have been a little unsteady due to some lingering painful bruises on my legs, but I held onto the railing and made it downstairs without incident. "See? Not a new injury in..."

I stopped when I realized that there was someone sitting on one of the stools at the counter whose presence was doing more to fill the room with light than the morning rays coming through the windows. "Gabriel! You came back!" *I hope you're not here to discourage me from going to Hell again, because you're way too late.*

He turned to see me, and what looked like the beginnings of smile on his face morphed into an expression of horror. "What happened?" He jumped up and crossed the room in two quick steps.

Bedlam appeared next to me. "Is he talking about your face or your hand?"

"Your hand? What's wrong with your hand?" Gabriel reached for my left hand and, seeing nothing amiss there, stretched to take my right.

I looked at Bedlam. "Can you go run that errand for me? I want to talk to Gabriel."

"Fine," Bedlam glanced at the angel who was now gaping in shock at the sigil on the back of my hand. "But I'm coming right back."

"Oh, Cassia." Gabriel looked up at me but didn't let go of my hand. "What have you done?"

I sighed. "Let me sit down, and I'll tell you. Unfortunately, some of these injuries are not just flesh wounds."

I hobbled over to one of the stools in front of the counter, and Gabriel sat down next to me. I told him everything that had happened to me in the last week or so, including the events before our argument. I filled him in on my journeys to Hell and the archdemons' prices for release. As my story progressed, I started to cry once again, and by the end of the tale, I could barely get the words out in between my sobs.

When I finished talking, Gabriel stood up wrapped both his arms around me. I couldn't get an exact thought from him, but the warmth and light of his presence washed over me. After a few minutes, I pulled away.

He considered me. "What do you want to do?"

"I want to have a normal day." I pulled out a napkin from the dispenser to dry my tears. "I want to pretend that nothing is going to happen today and hang out with you and Bedlam. I want one last happy day in the diner."

Gabriel nodded and sat back down, though I still couldn't tell what he was thinking. I had expected some kind of chastisement from him, but that didn't seem to be coming. On an ordinary day, I might fear that he didn't care about me; but today, I was grateful to not have another argument.

Bedlam appeared on the stool next to Gabriel. "Okay, mission accomplished. Sebastian is out one demon sigil." He took one look at my face, which I imagined was both red and puffy, and jumped out of his chair. "Are you upsetting her? Unacceptable! I challenge you to a duel!"

I laughed as much at Gabriel's inability to tell if the demon were serious as much as I did at Bedlam's joke. "I'm fine, Bedlam. No violence necessary."

The bell above the door rang, and Dwayne stepped in.

"Give me a minute, guys," I said.

Dwayne's eyes widened when he saw my face. "Wow, when Bedlam said you weren't feeling well, he wasn't kidding."

"No." I limped with Dwayne back to the kitchen. "So, something unexpected has come up, and I'm going away for a while."

Dwayne smiled. "Did you finally decide to go on that vacation?"

I made a sound somewhere between a laugh and a sob. "Something like that. Anyway, I'll be closing early tonight, and I won't need you to come in anymore. But I'll pay you a month's wages in advance, so you'll have time to find another job."

Dwayne nodded as Gabriel stuck his head into the kitchen. "Do you think you could make us some French toast?"

"I'll let you get to work." I followed Gabriel back into the main diner.

"—not sure that was a good idea," Bedlam was saying to Gabriel. "Have you had Dwayne's French toast? Even I can't eat it."

I put my finger to my lips. "Be quiet. He'll hear you. And it's not that bad."

Bedlam made a grumbling noise. "Fine. But if I'm eating that now, you are all eating peanut butter and bacon sandwiches for lunch."

I sat down in the stool I had vacated. "Don't I get to pick what I want to eat on my last day on earth?"

Bedlam spun around on his stool. "Well, Khet, if it is your last meal, which would you rather have? Something you've had a million times before, or one last creation that I invent for you? Keep in mind that either way, Dwayne will be the one making it."

I decided to let him have his way, and both the French toast and the peanut butter and bacon sandwiches were at least edible, though Bedlam swore the sandwiches would be better with crunchy peanut butter.

Other than that, the three of us did our best to have as ordinary a day as possible. Madame Zarita came in, and I had a conversation like the one I had with Dwayne with her, though she tried to pry more details out of me. A few customers did come in, but I didn't get to see Bedlam do any work because he convinced Gabriel to do it for him. Bedlam had the jukebox play my favorite songs, and he tried not to be too disappointed that I was not up for dancing. Gabriel sang along with some of the music, which I greatly appreciated, since he had a baritone voice like the angels of legend, one that even Bedlam stood still to listen to. I called my lawyer as soon as his office opened to ensure that all my worldly possessions were being left to one Brian Edward Lambert so that Bedlam would have my resources, provided he held on to the ID I had made for him. I also arranged to have Dwayne's mortgage paid off, since I was depriving him of his livelihood.

I tried to focus on every detail of the day so that I could carry the happy memories with me for as long as possible, once I was in the Abyss. I took in the smell of freshly brewed coffee as Bedlam upended a dozen sugar packets into a steaming mug, the upward quirk of Gabriel's lips when he didn't want to admit something Bedlam said was funny, the tone of Madame Zarita's voice as she called someone "dearie" and told him how to fix his life. It was all so ordinary and familiar, yet precious beyond measure.

At six o'clock, I flipped the sign on the diner to "Closed" and let Dwayne go with a large enough check that I hope he wasn't too angry with me for ending his employment.

"Okay, I guess it's about time for my last meal." I sat back down on my stool. "I'm thinking—"

"Pizza!" Bedlam stopped spinning on his stool and faced me. "With anchovies and onions. Ooh, and mushrooms. And maybe those sun-dried tomatoes."

"Bedlam! We decided that I get to pick."

Bedlam bounced up and down like a petulant child. "I know, but I remembered that pizza is only good when you have someone to order it with you. Otherwise you end up with leftovers, and pizza is not as good reheated. And no one's going to order pizza with me once you're gone."

"We should eat some of the food in the diner, rather than order in more food," Gabriel said. "It's going to go to waste, so we should at least try to eat some of that."

I looked at both of my friends in frustration. "What happened to whatever I wanted?"

"You may be right, Gabs," Bedlam said. "Given the Friday night delivery schedules, I'm not sure the food would get here in time for us to eat it."

"Seriously, guys—"

The jukebox started to play the opening howl of the Rolling Stones' "Sympathy for the Devil." Bedlam jumped up from his stool and pointed at the player. "That is not on my playlist!"

We swiveled our heads in the direction he was pointing, and all of us froze when we realized that another figure had joined us in the diner.

"I know," said the newcomer, whose mind I hadn't noticed over the din of Gabriel and Bedlam's. "But it is on mine."

Lucifer was an unassuming middle-aged man of average height and weight. His dark hair had enough grey in it to make him look distinguished but not elderly. He wore an old-fashioned grey pinstripe suit, complete with a double-breasted vest and pocket watch on a chain. In his hand he carried an antique cane that was more of an affectation than a support mechanism. I couldn't quite tell, but it looked like the ivory on the top of the cane was carved into the shape of a human skull. He smiled at the three of us, like an older relative taking pride in his descendants. The only thing that spoiled the effect was that no light escaped from his cold, black eyes.

"It's the only thing on your playlist. Your entire realm is one long Mick Jagger–a–thon." Bedlam snapped his fingers, and the jukebox switched its tune to the Charlie Daniels Band's "The Devil Went Down to Georgia."

He laughed. "A strangely apropos choice, Azazel, though I suspect you were trying to offend me." The three of us stared at him, waiting for him to explain his sudden arrival.

A full minute and a half passed.

"Well, I don't expect much from Azazel, but I would think that the rest of you would show some civility. Isn't anyone going to offer me a proper greeting?"

I exchanged glances with Gabriel and Bedlam and realized that it was my burden to play nice with one more archdemon this week. "Hello, Lucifer."

The Devil smiled back at me. "Hello, Cain."

CHAPTER 19

IKE EVERYONE ELSE, I HAD heard the story a number of times, and it went something like this: Adam and Eve, the first people God created, had two sons named Cain and Abel. God preferred Abel because he sacrificed animals instead of vegetables, and Cain was jealous because no one likes to be the less favored child. So one day Cain figured out a solution to the problem and murdered his brother. The next day, God asked Cain where Abel was, and Cain lied and said he had no idea. But God, being omniscient, knew he was lying, so he put a mark on Cain that no one would harm him and doomed him to walk isolated among mankind forever.

I didn't kill anybody, and I never had a brother. I'm pretty sure what happened wasn't the first murder, if you could even call it that. But there were enough similarities that I recognized the story as my own, and not just because the name of my town, which one might argue I had killed, was Abel.

Adam and Eve weren't my parents, but they were the names of two of the village elders who made the deal in the first place, so in that way I guess they were parents of everyone. Elder Rogan somehow got left out, but after eight thousand years in Hell, it couldn't make that much of a difference to him.

I never knew how the story got twisted around about me being envious of the town over God's favor, other than some later monotheists throwing in the God bit. But jealousy was a key part of the real story, too. Elders Adam, Eve, and Rogan were tired of our village placing last in every inter-village competition, and they wanted Abel to forever have something that the other towns didn't have: a psychic.

The lying to God part was mostly made up. He never talked to me at all. The only Heavenly being I discussed this with was Michael. When I walked out of my village, he asked me what happened, and I told him I had no idea, which was true enough. He said some nasty things to me and struck me on the arm with his flaming sword, leaving the only scar on my body that never healed. He said it marked me as cast out from Heaven, but I didn't see how it mattered, since I could never die.

As for the wandering forever alone among humanity— that I knew all too well.

I didn't commit the first murder. I didn't kill anyone, at least not directly. But on some level it was my fault that Lucifer chose to damn the town, and I carried that with me.

One day, when I was a small child, a stranger passed through Abel, and I was very excited about encountering a new mind. As soon as word spread that there was a traveler approaching the village, I ran ahead of the gathering crowd to walk with him into town.

At least, that was my plan. When I grew close to the man, however, I balked at what I was feeling from him: fear, loneliness, sadness, and anger to such strong degrees that I wondered that they could be described with the same words.

When the traveler saw me approaching him, he gave me a smile that I would have called kind, had I not felt the lack of emotion behind it. "Hello, little girl. My name is Lucifer. Tell me, what village do I have the honor of approaching?" *If there could be any honor in approaching something so contemptible as a human village.*

I stared into his black eyes and tried to decide whether I should speak to his words or his thoughts. "We call the village Abel." I pointed to the three people at the front of the crowd. "Those are our leaders, there."

We walked up the hill toward the village in silence, and I considered what to say to him. Something weighed greatly on his mind, but I didn't know whether I should reach out to help this enigmatic stranger.

He must have grown tired of watching me stare at him because a few minutes later he said, "Is something bothering you, little girl? Out with it."

I still wasn't sure I should trust him but decided that my words couldn't hurt. "You're worried that you've done something so horrible that your father won't love you anymore. It's not true."

Lucifer stopped in his tracks and peered at me. "And how do you know that?"

"I know because you know. You are thinking that it's possible he will never forgive you. But really, you know that there is nothing you can do that will stop him from loving you."

For some reason, that caused his level of ire to rise. "We'll see about that." He resumed his stride toward the village at a faster pace.

"Welcome to the village of Abel!" Elder Rogan approached him with open arms. "We are always pleased to welcome travelers and hear their news from other villages!" He glanced down at me. "I see you have met little Cain. She is our pride and joy, though she can be overly high-spirited at times. Run along and play, little one, and let us see to our guest."

I hesitated a moment, wondering if I should explain the feeling of discomfort that the stranger gave me. But the leaders smiled and didn't notice anything amiss, so I put my trust in them as I always did, as everyone did. I ran to find my friends in the crowd, not knowing it was the last choice I would make with a free soul. I wouldn't know that for another ten years.

Eight thousand years later, give or take a few centuries, Lucifer—also known as Sammael, Satan, the devil, the Morning Star, and a million other names—stood in my diner after revealing my greatest shame to my two oldest friends. Lucifer never did anything without a purpose, but if he expected either of my friends to change their opinions of me based on my name, he was disappointed.

Bedlam waved a hand at one of the tables. "Pull up a chair, Luci! We're having a waiting-for-Azrael party, and we could use some help planning the menu."

"Sadly, I cannot stay long, Azazel." Lucifer took a few steps toward us, his cane clicking against the linoleum as he walked. "And though I do so much hate to be the bearer of bad news, I have come to inform you that Azrael will not be making an appearance at your festivities this evening."

Bedlam slouched on his stool. "This whole 'using our real names' business would make a lot more sense if you went by yours, Sammy-boy." His head snapped back to look at Lucifer. "Hold on a minute. Did you say that Azrael *isn't* coming?"

I glanced down at my hand. The mark was still there and looked the same, so far as I could see.

I knew it, thought Gabriel, and both Lucifer and I turned our heads to look at him.

Lucifer took a few more steps forward to look Gabriel in the eye. "Interesting that it was the noble angel who could foresee the outcome of a devil's deal."

Gabriel shrugged and met Lucifer's gaze. "Bedlam believes that angels can change. And Cassia, even with all her powers, is still mortal. But I know that if there is one constant in the universe, it is the Morning Star's pride. There was no way you were going to let Cassia negate the spirit of your contract."

"Indeed." Lucifer did his best not to reveal his discomposure at Gabriel's assessment. He turned his regard back to me. "For those of you still not quite up to speed, the matter is very simple. Azrael has laid claim to your soul, and she is quite correct in thinking that I cannot override that. However, she would need to be in a position to collect your soul, and I have ensured that she will not be able to do that for the foreseeable future." *It's such an exquisite pleasure, sending my demons out into the Abyss. Really, I should do it more often.*

I crossed my arms. "That's not right, Lucifer. It's my choice what happens to my soul."

"Yes, Cain, of course it is." Lucifer reached out and put a hand on my shoulder. I wrested it free. "But, sadly, it is not your choice what happens to your *life*. And I suppose that I cannot stop you from returning to Hell of your own accord, but trust me when I say that I can and will find increasingly unpleasant ways of returning you to your body. I will not have you sullying a deal that I made in good faith."

"Don't worry." I didn't look at Bedlam, but I felt him glaring at me, as if he could force me to acquiesce to his wishes if he stared at me hard enough. "She won't be returning to Hell anytime in the near future."

"I trust that she won't." Lucifer turned and walked back in the direction of the jukebox, but after a moment stopped and looked back at me. "And to set your mind at ease on another matter, I have made it clear to Azrael that she is to abide by the rules of her own contract, and the boy over whom that scuffle began is not to be harmed."

I had mixed feelings about the new arrangement. I felt that by not holding up my end of the contract, I was cheating, but it also seemed pointless to go to Hell without Azrael's enforcement, especially if Lucifer would just send me back to Earth. And I wouldn't wish the Abyss on anyone, even someone as unpleasant as Azrael. Besides, she would no doubt get out eventually, and Lucifer and I would both have to deal with the consequences of that.

Lucifer seemed about to disappear, but I called him back. "How did you even find out about the deal? I made it less than twenty-four hours ago."

Bedlam snorted. "I know the answer to that one. Like every smart kid, Meph is a brownnosing teacher's pet. He tattled, didn't he?"

"Quite. Now, if you'll excuse me, I really do have an entire underworld to run, and there is only so much time in the world."

After Lucifer left, the diner was so quiet I heard the drip of the faucet in the kitchen sink. I couldn't think of the best way to break the silence. What do you say to your two best friends when they've been anticipating your death all day and now know you are the inspiration for a Biblical villain?

Yeah, this isn't awkward or anything, Bedlam thought.

I glanced at the clock on the wall. "Well, since it seems like I am stuck in this mortal coil for a while longer, I might as well get on with my life." I stood up and limped over to the door. "I told Sebastian that I would come see him tonight, and I might as well go over and explain things to him."

Gabriel indicated that he had an errand to run, and Bedlam muttered that he needed to do something related to tree frogs. So after they both disappeared, I turned off the lights and went out to catch the SEPTA bus.

CHAPTER 20

A T 7:45 P.M., I RANG the doorbell of a well-kept brick row house. *I hope this is the right place. I can't believe Bedlam lost Sebastian's address.* After a minute, a college-aged girl answered the door and looked at me with a mixture of shock and fear. *What? I'm not that intimidating. Oh, right, ripped apart by wild dogs.*

"Hi." I made my best attempt at a smile. "I'm looking for Sebastian. Is this the right house?"

The girl's eyes narrowed. "Are you Azrael?"

Phew. Right place. "No. I'm Carrie."

"Okay." She stepped back to let me in. "I didn't think you were. Sebastian said Azrael would be the most beautiful woman I ever saw, and that's clearly not you." She clapped her hand over her mouth. "I mean, I don't mean that you look bad or anything, just that..."

"I look as though I've had better days?" I gave her a more natural smile to reassure her that I was not offended.

She nodded. "Right. Plus, your eyes aren't cold and hollow. I'm Felicity, by the way. I think Sebastian is expecting you. I'll go get him."

I stood in the foyer of Sebastian's house. Several pairs of sneakers lined the wall at the bottom of the stairs, and a set of keys and a purse sat on a wooden table next to the door. On the wall hung a slightly crooked portrait of a mother, a father, and three smiling children. It was such an ordinary family scene. Even though we didn't have photographs or keys back then, the scene reminded me of my home before I became immortal, of the normal life I used to have.

Sebastian came down the stairs and greeted me with nervous smile. "I'm so glad you came, Carrie." *Why is she here? I thought Bedlam said...*

"Hi." I gave an awkward wave. "I wanted to make sure that you were okay."

"Yeah, I think so." He walked the rest of the way down the stairs. "Your friend Bedlam stopped by before. He said I didn't have to worry about Azrael anymore, though he seemed displeased about it. Was he... was he wrong? Is that why you're here?" *Was it some kind of sick joke?*

"Oh, no!" I shook my head. "No, Azrael isn't going to be bothering anyone for a while, I don't think. I came by to make sure that you knew that."

Except, looking at him now, I wasn't sure at all why I had come. A few days ago, when we had gone out and when he had visited me when I was hurt, I had felt closer to him than I had felt to any human in a long time. But now, even though he was the same person he had been when he walked into my diner a few weeks ago, all connection between us was gone.

He reached out to straighten the crooked picture. "What happened? Do you know? Was it even real?"

I had intended to tell him the truth, but I found that I wasn't able to. I put my right hand behind my back so that he would not see the sigil burned there. "What do you think?"

He took a deep breath and looked away from me. "I'm starting to doubt whether any of it was real. I mean, it seems so absurd, selling my soul and stuff. But I can't believe that you would lie to me. And Felicity did get better. So I don't know. Felicity thinks that God saw what was happening, saw that I was a good and honest person, and decided to intervene." He met my eyes. "Is that what happened?"

He wanted to believe his theory, and I found I had something else to envy him for, the belief in a loving God who took care of His children. And despite all the trouble I had gone to in order to save his soul, I couldn't lead him to doubt that. "God works in mysterious ways."

I looked at him, and for once I almost felt as if I could see his future. He would travel the globe for a while, helping people in need, but eventually he would come home to his family and fulfill his dream of going to law school. He would marry some nice girl who probably wouldn't deserve him but would love him anyway, and they would have children whom they would see laugh and grow and have children of their own. And he would look back at this time in his life and only remember the miracle of his sister's recovery and forget about me and Bedlam and Azrael and all the darkness that shadowed his past few years.

And as for me, I had achieved my goal. I had saved his soul. And now it was time for me to go.

Back in the diner the next day, I contemplated some changes to the menu and hummed along with the Bach that Bedlam had left on the jukebox for me. I felt the light and warmth of Gabriel's presence as he appeared in the diner. I looked up to smile at him but felt my face fall when I saw his resolute countenance and investigated the thoughts behind it.

"You're going back." I paused to cover the catch in my voice. "To Heaven. You're going back to Heaven."

"It's time," he said. "Michael is right. The balance is going to shift soon. Or maybe it has already started. I need to be where I can do the most good."

"Oh."

He's right, part of me said. *If change is coming, Heaven is going to need all the power it can get.*

But the rest of me asked, *What am I going to do when he's gone?*

"Cassia?"

"Hmm?" I didn't look at him.

"It's going to be okay." He leaned forward to try to meet my eyes. "Whatever is coming, we'll take care of it. You don't have to worry."

I wanted to tell him that nothing would be okay for me, not if he was gone, but it would do no good. "I know, Gabriel."

"Thank you, Cassia. For being there for me. For everything." With a flash of blinding light, he disappeared.

I waited until I was absolutely sure that he was gone and collapsed on my knees behind the counter. And for what seemed like the hundredth time that week, I began to cry.

At some point, Bedlam returned to the diner, and he didn't even have to ask. He knew that after everything that I had faced in the past few weeks, there was only one thing that could make me cry even harder. He didn't say anything, just sat down next to me and pulled me into his arms. At some point, he took me upstairs and made me go to bed, letting me cry on his shoulder all the while. At least until he fell asleep. Then he was stealing the covers, per usual.

I woke as the first rays of light were peeking through my curtains, and somehow all the tears were cried out of me. I showered and put on my favorite red skirt, then went over to pull open the curtains.

Bedlam made a groaning noise as the sun hit his face. He sat up halfway and put his hand over his eyes to block the light.

I put my hands on my hips. "I have made a decision."

"Okay..." For someone who didn't need any sleep, Bedlam could be awfully persnickety about getting up in the morning.

I reached into my closet to pull out a pair of shoes that

matched my skirt. "I'm closing the diner on Mondays. And I am going to go out and do things. With people. I can't really do too much yet, but today I am at least going to go over to the Franklin Institute and look at all the exhibits I missed the other day. And next week, I am going to go buy some new clothes. And shoes. Ones that are impractical but cute. And match a new outfit. And then, when I'm feeling better, you and I are going out dancing."

His brow furrowed. "We are?"

"Yes." I looked over at him. "It's you and me, right? That's what you said."

He grinned at me, and in that smile I saw the potential for mayhem that only the demon of chaos could create. "Right."

AUTHOR'S NOTE

There are many books that strive for authentic historical accuracy in all things.

Oracle of Philadelphia is not one of those books.

This is not to say that I did not spend hours on the Internet trying to find authentic names for each historical period or use up many of my minutes on my cell phone calling my historian sister and asking questions like "Did they have books in ancient Rome?" (They didn't) and "What about brooms?" (Those, they had). Where possible, I strove for historical accuracy.

However, any modern English description of a historical time period is going to be a translation of old language and culture. Where it made the story better (or one of Bedlam's jokes funnier), I took some liberties with my translation. So while Bedlam might not have insisted on going to see the world's longest aqueduct, he would have done something to make the trip longer and more exciting for him.

So if you see something that seems anachronistic or historically inaccurate, I wrote it that way in the name of more entertaining fantasy fiction, not out of any kind of ignorance or disrespect of history.

ACKNOWLEDGMENTS

Thanks to my alpha readers: Stephanie, Kevin, and Mom/ Virginia. You read my book in its rawest form and still believed it was worth something.

Thanks to my beta readers: Anne, Jason, Deena, Gwyn, and Dad/Steve. If you had not supported my book, it might not be where it is today. If I forgot anyone, you may smack me around later.

Thanks to my editors: Michelle, Misti, Kris, and the rest of the Red Adept team. Without you, my book would have been very different and mostly worse.

Special thanks to Stephanie and Greg for being my resident Philly experts.

And infinite thanks to the Internet for always being there when I had questions like "What was a common girl's name in Ancient Greece beginning with 'C'?" and "Did they have onions in Ancient Mesopotamia?" I don't know how people wrote books before you existed.

ABOUT ELIZABETH CORRIGAN

Elizabeth has degrees in English and psychology and has spent several years working as a data analyst in various branches of the healthcare industry. When she's not hard at work on her next novel, Elizabeth enjoys singing, reading teen vampire novels, and making Sims of her characters.

She drinks more Diet Coke than is probably optimal for the human body and is pathologically afraid of bees. She lives in Maryland with two cats and a purple Smart Car.

33549653R00132

Made in the USA
Middletown, DE
17 July 2016